"Every time you look at me, I know that you're judging me."

"That's not true." H... her. "Since I was thi... to notice me becaus...

When he reached her, he grazed his hands over her arms, loosening her grip until her hands dangled at her side. He entwined his fingers with hers. "I don't know how judgment can shine from my eyes when love warms my heart every time I look at you. Don't think all of your rebuffs and teasing didn't hurt me over the years. I kept following you around, hoping you'd change your mind and like me."

A sly twinkle winked from his brown eyes, his lips curved into that familiar grin. This time the slight curl of his lips didn't raise her ire. The dim glow of the bunkhouse cast a different light on his smile, making Jennifer realize it wasn't cocky but apprehensive.

"Did you just say that you loved me?" Her voice whispered of disbelief.

ROSE ROSS ZEDIKER

lives in rural Elk Point, South Dakota, with her husband of twenty-eight years. Their grown son has started a family of his own. Rose works full-time for an investment firm and writes during the evening or weekends. Some of her pastimes include reading, sewing, embroidery, quilting and spoiling her granddaughters.

Besides writing inspirational romance novels, Rose has many publishing credits in the Christian children's genre. She is a member of American Christian Fiction Writers. Visit Rose on the Web at www.roserosszediker.blogspot.com.

ROSE ROSS ZEDIKER

Wedding on the Rocks

HEARTSONG
PRESENTS

Recycling programs
for this product may
not exist in your area.

™ LOVE INSPIRED BOOKS

ISBN-13: 978-0-373-48658-8

WEDDING ON THE ROCKS

www.LoveInspiredBooks.com

Printed in U.S.A.

For we live by faith, not by sight.
—*2 Corinthians* 5:7

For Mike, with love.

Chapter 1

The sweat-soaked silk fabric of Jennifer Edwards's blouse stuck to her back. The tremors in her arms and legs became full-fledged shakes.

"Hold steady!" Eldon, their ranch foreman, commanded.

"I'm trying." The rattle of the chain mocked her efforts to assist with pulling a calf. She lifted her right foot and stepped back. The baggy leg of her dad's coveralls, which she'd slipped on to protect her designer suit, fell catching the fabric between her spiked boot heel and the barn floor. There was no way she'd hold her footing now. Her ankle boots, the perfect accessory to her designer suit in Chicago, weren't cut out for ranch work in South Dakota.

She should have kicked them off when Eldon met her at the rental car shouting, "We have a cow in trouble! We need to pull her calf." She wished her dad was here to help. Sadness washed through her. He might never have the ability to do ranch work again.

Please God, don't let our efforts fail. The prayer from
her youth automatically popped into her mind. Through
the years she'd played nursemaid to several orphaned
calves whose moms had given their lives for their babies.

Just like yours. Jennifer's heart twisted in her chest.
She swallowed hard. Thirty years old and the hurt still
sucked at her heart. No matter how hard she fought it,
the pain's pull devoured her being like quicksand captured a victim.

"Where is that vet?" Jennifer bent her knees deeper
in hopes of relieving some of the stress on her revolting
muscles.

The purr of an ATV engine sounded in the distance.
No wonder it had taken the vet so long. How fast could
an ATV go? Forty? Forty-five? The reverberations grew
louder and finally stopped by the barn door.

Jennifer waited until the vet cut the engine. "Hurry!"
she shouted then drew a deep breath. Would oxygen help
steady her muscles? Knees bent, she angled back, thinking her body weight would help hold the chain steady.
Instead the force proved too much for the skinny spiked
heel of her free foot. It buckled.

She angled her foot in an effort to keep her footing, but
the slick sole slid on the wooden floor pushing her toes
full force into the cramped pointed toe of her boot. Pain
shot up her foot as her toes pinched together, and her leg
flew out from under her.

"Eldon, I'm sorry." Her apology puffed out while her
body tumbled sideways. Her bottom thumped to the floor.
Her trapped foot turned sideways. She closed her eyes,
biting her upper lip to keep her cry of pain inside. She
braced for the backward fall when the chain slackened.
Instead her body jerked forward, remaining in a precari-
ous sitting position.

What was going on? Had Eldon grabbed hold of her chain with one hand? Impossible. She opened her eyes and looked directly into the knee creases on denim jeans. The vet. He must have grabbed the grip on the chain. She drew in a deep breath. The calf might survive.

Slowly, Jennifer straightened her bent leg, ignoring the throbbing in her left hip, which had taken the brunt of her fall. Any fast movement could disrupt the pull of the chain. With gritted teeth, she rolled so her weight was evenly distributed on her bottom.

"Am I glad to see you." Eldon's deep exhale indicated he'd feared the worst for the cow and calf. "Give another pull."

Jennifer used her hands to scoot back out of the way of the high lace-up work boots that were backing toward her.

"Finally. What took you so long, Doc?" Eldon asked.

"Two bull buffalo jumped a fence and are standing in the highway." The deep baritone of Doc Kane's voice came from behind them.

Jennifer looked over her shoulder at the man who was just arriving. If the vet was behind her, then who was in front of her? She started at the bottom of the worn leather boots, letting her eyes travel upward. Leather mid-calf lace-up boots. Blue jeans. Gauzy white shirt. Brown fedora. Young Indy? Couldn't be. Could it?

Her gaze roamed over the stranger before her. The Brett Lange she grew up with was only an inch or two taller than her and stick-thin. Football players would envy this guy's broad square shoulders. He was easily six feet tall. No, it couldn't be Brett Lange.

"Whose buffalo? Which highway?" Eldon's voice broke through Jennifer's confusion.

"Matthew's and two-twelve." Doc Kane moved to the cow, studying the progress of the birth.

Jennifer jerked her head toward Eldon. "Buffalo? Dad has buffalo? Since when?"

"Brett, give me a good strong pull on that chain to get the right shoulder out."

"Eldon?" Jennifer wanted an answer. It was bad enough she had to deal with cattle. She didn't know a thing about buffalo.

"Now is not the time." Eldon furrowed his brow. Her dad's best friend's brown eyes sent a silent message: *You would've known that if your visits had been more frequent than a couple of days every other holiday.*

"Slip out of that loop. You're in Brett's way." Eldon turned his attention back to Doc. "They gonna make it?"

"Looks good so far. Jennifer, I didn't realize that was you. What are you doing down there on the floor?"

Jennifer started to respond but caught the sly smile forming on Eldon's lips.

"Citified shoes." Eldon didn't even try to muffle his chuckle.

Anger bubbled Jennifer's blood. She pushed to her feet, balancing on the toe of her right foot, and wiggled free of the chain. She limped around the man standing before her. It was Brett Lange all grown up. She'd know those brown eyes anywhere.

She placed her hands on her hips. "I don't see what's so funny about me falling."

"Nothing." Brett cleared his throat, but the corner of his mouth turned up into a cocky grin and his brown eyes reflected merriment, his words and expression definitely not in agreement.

Jennifer snorted. "What are you doing here anyway?"

Doc cleared his throat. "Although it's good to see you, Jennifer, we're kind of busy here. Think you could rustle us up some coffee?"

A gentle dismissal. That was Doc, and he was right. Losing a cow or calf or both wasn't the way she wanted to start her promise to her dad.

Jennifer turned on her good heel and, holding her right heel high to keep it even with her booted foot, she walked toward the side entry and slipped through the single barn door. Holding it open a crack, she rested her head on the rough exterior of the barn.

It'd been a long, stressful day full of surprises. She'd made a promise that she might not be able to keep. Her taxed muscles throbbed. She'd make the coffee in a minute. She needed to know the outcome of this last surprise. *Please, Lord, let it be good.*

"Eldon, give me a strong pull to get that other shoulder out. Looking good, boys." Doc's instruments clinked while he worked. "Almost got it. Why was Jennifer dressed like that to pull a calf?"

"She's not a country girl anymore, Doc. Since she moved away she's become all citified." Eldon didn't disguise his disgust.

Brett's laughter erupted in the barn.

Anger made Jennifer's muscles tremble. She'd had enough of Eldon's digs at her lifestyle. She slapped the barn door shut, hoping the men inside would know that she heard their comments.

She turned and took a step, forgetting the broken heel of her boot, and stumbled. Trying to regain her balance, the toe of her boot caught in the long fabric of the coveralls. She waved her arms in a fight to remain upright. Her formfitting jacket ripped and she went crashing to the hard ground, her hands and knees smacking into the cool spring soil.

Jennifer moaned and tears formed in her eyes. She never should have promised to run the ranch. But how could she say no to her Dad when he lay in the hospital partially paralyzed from a stroke and worried about his livelihood? She hoped he'd recover after a couple of weeks of rehabilitation. If he didn't, she'd be out of vacation time.

She wiped the back of her gloved hands over her eyes and pushed herself up to one knee.

"Are you all right?"

A strong arm looped around her waist. She leaned into Brett's solid body as he lifted her to her feet.

Jennifer stood for a few moments until she realized that Brett's arms were still holding her secure. She threw his hand off of her shoulder. "I don't need your help." Jennifer swiped her hands over the dirt on the knees of the coveralls.

"Really? Seems to me I'm always rescuing you."

Not only did the cocky grin appear but Brett taunted her with raised eyebrows. He'd crossed his arms in front of his chest and his brown eyes dared her to disagree.

Jennifer unzipped the coveralls and slipped her arms out. Gravity pulled the heavy denim to the ground. Gingerly, she stepped out of them. She wasn't going to fall again, at least not in front of Faith, South Dakota's own Indiana Jones wannabe.

The memory turned the corners of Jennifer's lips into a sly smile. The nickname she'd bestowed upon Brett had caused him a lot of torment growing up. Well-deserved torment in her opinion. What senior girl wanted to be pestered by a sophomore? Although his tagalong nature came in handy once.

"Really." She'd met his challenge. Jennifer lifted her right leg to unzip the broken boot. She teetered on the remaining spiked heel that inched its way into the damp spring soil but managed to free herself from her broken footwear without toppling over.

"See?" Jennifer held up her trophy. She surveyed the damage. The four-inch heel had snapped in two. She'd have to make a trip to the shoe repair shop when she went back to Chicago. "Now don't start pestering me. Let's not repeat the past."

"Pestering you?" Brett put a hand to his heart. "That hurts. I idolized you. The girl with everything."

Jennifer rolled her eyes. "You only say that because the ranch is filled with rock crags and dirt." Jennifer lowered her eyes. Brett had everything she longed to have—a mother—and he knew it. She always enjoyed Mrs. Lange's company, but Brett's jealous bone showed when his mother paid attention to someone else's child.

She rested her left leg on her right knee to remove the other boot. It was much easier to balance on a flat stocking foot. The cold, damp earth soaked through her socks, soothing the ache of her fashion-abused feet. She dropped the boots on the coveralls.

Brett held his palms up and shrugged. "What more does a person need? Besides—" Brett nodded his head toward her boot and pointed to her jacket back "—they last longer than superficial items."

Her shoulders sagged. She'd forgotten that her jacket had ripped. Although she'd purchased the expensive suit in a consignment boutique, Brett didn't need to know that. Add tailor shop to her Chicago to-do list.

"Since when are shoes and clothes in the superficial category? I believe they are necessities." Same old Brett, picking at her clothes, shoes and makeup choices.

"Practical clothes and shoes are necessities. Those—" Brett waved a hand up and down through the air "—are just window dressing to hide behind."

Jennifer ripped the Velcro tab free on the work gloves, slipped them off and watched them land on the growing mound of clothes. She surveyed her French manicure. Her nails had made it through this test.

She turned her attention back to Brett and narrowed her eyes. "Are you trying to provoke me?" If so, it was working. She took a deep breath before removing her jacket and dropped it on top of the stack on the ground. He might not have changed, but she had and this was her opportunity to prove it.

"Obviously, my outfit is impractical for ranch work in Faith, South Dakota, but it's the standard dress code for a columnist in Chicago, Illinois."

Jennifer flashed Brett her practiced business smile. "You should get out and see more of the world. See for yourself that fashion consists of more than copying a movie hero's costumes." Okay, maybe she hadn't changed that much.

"Do you consider that an insult? Do you know how much money those movies grossed? That's not counting the television series." Brett moved close, his shadow shading Jennifer from the afternoon sun.

She shivered. certain it was from the cool spring air seeping through her damp silk blouse. Slowly she tilted her head up. He *had* grown.

His fingers glided up her neck leaving a trail of tingles on her skin. Stopping under her chin, he gently pushed her jaw, closing her gaping mouth.

He searched her face. Appreciation flickered through his eyes. "Just so you know, I studied abroad, and this is the standard dress code for a professor of archeology when he's on a dig. You don't have the market cornered on following your dream."

Jennifer licked her lips, expecting that at any moment his might descend upon hers.

Her simple gesture sparked amusement in his eyes,

punctuated by a cocky smile. He pulled back. "Pestering, huh? I don't think so."

He chuckled and stepped back. "In case you're wondering, the calf and cow both made it, and eavesdropping is rude." He turned and walked toward the ATV.

He straddled the seat and turned back to Jennifer. "If I were you I'd get changed. Rounding up buffalo isn't an occupation that requires a silk-and-tweed outfit." His chuckles turned into guffaws.

The roar of the all-terrain's engine covered up Brett's taunting laughter. Humiliation surged through Jennifer. Why had she thought he'd kiss her? Had she wanted him to? She pursed her traitorous lips. She did not want Brett Lange to kiss her, not twelve years ago and certainly not now.

She kicked at the pile of clothes before bending and scooping them up into her arms. She walked to her rental car, which sat beside the ranch house. The square two-story turn-of-the-century home appeared withered; its white paint cracked and peeling away from the siding, gave it a worn-out look.

Jennifer surveyed her attire. The same could be said of her. Why had she promised to take care of the ranch? Her mind flashed to the image of her dad's pleading eyes. His struggle to voice his thoughts through stroke-induced partial paralysis. That's why. She wanted him to relax and get better, so she'd made a promise that might end up idle if her promotion at work came through. She hoped she could stay until he recovered. She watched a dirt cloud form behind the departing ATV. But she wasn't staying one day more.

Chapter 2

The departing ATV headed toward the western pasture of the Eddy Ranch. Why was Brett going that way? His parents lived in Faith.

Eldon and Doc's voices drifted from the barn like wind chimes caught by a soft breeze. Coffee.

Jennifer grabbed several shopping bags from the backseat of the rental car before hurrying into the house. She set the bags beside the door, then dropped the bundle of clothes on the laundry room floor just off of the kitchen.

Once the coffee was brewing, Jennifer, bags in hand, headed to her childhood bedroom to change into the new work clothes she'd bought at the Rushmore Mall before leaving Rapid City for the one-hundred-mile trip to Faith.

Between the two Western stores, she'd outfitted herself with rugged boots, jeans, T-shirts and soft Western-cut chambray shirts. She'd had no idea when she left Chicago that she'd be running the ranch for a while. The trendy apparel she'd packed for her short vacation was useless for ranch work. Her ruined jacket and boots were proof of that.

When Jennifer returned to the kitchen, Eldon and Doc were leaning against opposite kitchen counters sipping their coffee. Eldon lifted a full mug, holding it out to Jennifer.

"Better." He gave her a slight nod of approval.

Jennifer ran her hands down the stiff denim of her new jeans before she took the offered cup. The square-cut jean jacket and soft T-shirt underneath allowed ample room for movement. The Fatbaby cowgirl boots comforted her achy feet with their wide toes and rubber soles, and the hot pink suede shaft with decorative stitching satisfied her fashion sense.

"Why does Dad run buffalo?" Jennifer took a sip of the coffee. Would the same skills used for cattle apply to buffalo?

"There's a demand for bison meat because it's leaner. Market prices are high. Upkeep of the herd is easy."

"Unless you have short fencing." Doc Kane set his empty cup on the counter turning toward Jennifer. "Bull buffalo can make a standing six-foot jump if they want to. Got to keep them out of that southern pasture. The highway's a dangerous place for buffalo."

"I still don't understand why Dad would want a buffalo herd in addition to running horses and cattle."

Eldon's coffee cup clicked against the countertop when he set it down. "Bad economy affects all business. Your Dad is trying anything to keep the ranch profitable—or break even."

Jennifer's heart dropped to her stomach. "Is Dad in financial trouble?" She looked from Eldon to Doc Kane and back to Eldon.

Eldon's somber brown eyes bore into her. "Not yet, he's willing to try new things."

"Like raising bison?"

"That and renting out land."

"Dad's renting to other ranchers?"

"Not exactly." Eldon crossed his arms over his chest, rocking from his heels to his toes and back again.

"Is my girl here and nobody told me?" Cynthia Clearwater burst through the mud-porch door and entered the kitchen. Her arms outstretched, waiting to wrap Jennifer in a hug.

"Cynthia." Jennifer met her midway, enveloping the woman in her arms.

After a brief moment, Cynthia pulled Jennifer to arm's length. "The city treats you well."

"Not as well as country life treats you—you haven't aged a bit since the last time I was home." Traditional Lakota beadwork decorated the barrettes that held Cynthia's long salt-and-pepper hair away from her face. Jennifer's pixie cut no longer allowed her to wear the hand-beaded hair decorations Cynthia made her over the years. But she still cherished them and kept them in a drawer in her jewelry armoire.

"You always were a sweet child, but I'm not getting younger." Cynthia shrugged.

"She is getting feistier though." Eldon hooted at his own joke. He tucked his gray ponytail into his cowboy hat before lifting it back onto his head. "Well, got to round up those stray buffalo."

"Want me to stick around and help you?" Doc asked.

"No, Jennifer and I can do it."

"No ranch work on her first day home." Cynthia pointed a warning finger at Eldon.

"Too late. I tried to help pull a calf." Jennifer's voice

trailed off. It really was a good thing Brett had stepped in because by the sounds of it, the ranch couldn't afford to lose any livestock.

Cynthia turned to Eldon. "Why didn't you call me?"

Eldon ground the pointed tip of his cowboy boot into the kitchen tile. "You were hauling hay to the cattle in the west pasture. You wouldn't have made it in time."

"Why were you hauling hay? Where are the hired hands?" Jennifer asked. Her dad usually hired one full-time hand and one part-timer during the winter months. More during peak seasons of the summer.

Eldon and Cynthia kept their eyes locked. Doc looked everywhere but at Jennifer.

Jennifer placed her hand on Cynthia's arm and answered her own question. "There's no money to hire ranch hands."

The Clearwaters, in sync after so many years of marriage, shook their heads in confirmation.

Jennifer sighed. Why hadn't Dad shared this with her? Had the financial struggle contributed to his stroke?

"You men go on and round up that buffalo. Call Brett if you need help. He won't refuse. He's a good man. He was a good boy." Cynthia locked eyes with Jennifer on the last statement, punctuating it with a nod of her head.

That simple gesture spoke more than words. Eldon and Doc didn't seem to notice the silent conversation going on between Jennifer and Cynthia. Cynthia knew what had really happened in the winter of Jennifer's senior year. No doubt she held Brett in high regard for his part in it.

Eldon poured the remaining coffee into a thermos. "We should be back by suppertime." He pecked a kiss on Cynthia's cheek; then he and Doc disappeared through the mud porch.

Jennifer busied herself starting another pot of coffee. "How is Lance?"

"Our son is well. He works at keeping our traditions alive. Not in the radical way of his youth, though." Cynthia raised an eyebrow. Perhaps she only suspected about the incident that happened so many years ago. Jennifer danced around the subject.

"Does he come home—I mean out to the ranch much?"

Lance had been her best friend growing up, since Eldon and Cynthia lived in the hired hands house about a mile from the main ranch house. That friendship cooled midway through their senior year.

"Every couple of months. He's made a life in the city. Although Rapid City is much closer than Chicago."

Jennifer pulled the coffeepot mid-brew and poured two mugs of coffee. After returning the pot to the coffeemaker, she slid onto a stool at the kitchen island. Cynthia joined her.

"Are we the only ranch in trouble?"

"No. Many are worse off than Eddy Ranch. Matthew and Eldon aren't prideful. They will try anything to keep the ranch solvent. So far, it's worked."

"But you shouldn't be throwing hay bales. They're too heavy for women."

Cynthia chuckled. "You had trouble throwing bales because you're petite. Some women throw them better than a man. However, Matthew switched to round bales. All I have to do is start the tractor, push the bale hauling fork into the round bale, make sure it's secure and drive it out to where it needs to be dropped."

"So you're okay with doing ranch work?" Jennifer took a drink of her coffee.

"This land may belong to your family but it's my home and I'll do whatever I can to save it. Besides, without several people to cook for and clean up after, I have plenty of time to help out although that will change in a few weeks." Cynthia smiled.

Jennifer knitted her brows in confusion. "I thought we weren't hiring hands."

"We aren't."

"Then who are you cooking for?"

"Brett's kids."

"Brett's married?" No wonder he found her earlier actions amusing.

"No, not married. For the past few years, he's hosted a two-week dig for inner-city kids. They stay out here on the ranch." Cynthia's eyes sparkled. "It's so much fun to see the wonder on their faces with each new discovery about ranch life, especially on a starlit night."

"Is that why he's out here? Scoping out the rocky bluffs to see where he wants to dig?" Jennifer wanted to roll her eyes. Brett had become enamored with archeology when a Tyrannosaurus Rex fossil was discovered on a neighboring ranch about twenty years before. Unlike Brett, she had been sure that was a once-in-a-lifetime find.

"Hmm…not really. Eldon didn't tell you?"

Jennifer shook her head. If he wasn't scoping rock formations, what was he doing on their ranch?

"He won a research grant for a six-month dig. He rented the west pasture.…"

"Great," Jennifer interrupted. "Indy's going to come out to the ranch every day." What had she gotten herself into making that promise?

"I don't think you understand. Brett," Cynthia enunciated his given name, "lives here."

A laugh snorted out of Jennifer. "He stays in a tent on the dig site in the rocky crags where rattlesnakes live? I can't believe it. He's afraid of snakes." She'd dubbed him

Indy not because of his interest in fossils but because he was deathly afraid of any kind of snake.

"Everyone has fears." Cynthia's tone warned Jennifer that she wasn't amused by Jennifer's attitude. "Brett lives here, in the main house. He sleeps in the guest room."

"Well, Dad may have thought that arrangement was okay, but I don't. He's going to have live with his parents and drive out every day."

"The agreement between Brett and Matthew included room and board."

"Contracts can be broken."

"Not this one."

Jennifer jumped, turning on the stool toward the door. Brett stood in the entryway between the kitchen and mud porch, his broad shoulders filling the small span of space. She hadn't heard the ATV engine approach the house.

"You can't stay here."

"Yes, I can. I have a legal document to prove it." Brett's eyes roved over her. His cocky smile appeared. "Finally in sensible clothes, I see."

Jennifer's eyes narrowed. Her rapid heartbeat echoed in her ears. She wanted to blame anger for the sudden speeding of her heart rate, but it was the appreciation that flickered in Brett's eyes. This was why he couldn't stay.

"I promised Dad that I'd run the ranch during his recovery. You'll have to live with your parents until Dad comes home."

"I already paid Matthew's asking price for the dig and it included room and board. I'm staying." Brett moved closer, bracing his arms on the counter and leaning toward Jennifer.

Jennifer inhaled a deep breath to steady her racing heart. Soft scents of spring, damp gravel and new grass drifted off Brett, filling her lungs. It lured her closer. The exact reason why she had to convince him that living here was a bad idea.

"I'll give you part of your money back if you go live with your parents for the remainder of my stay."

Cynthia patted Jennifer's back. "You can't do that. The money's already spent."

Brett felt sorry for Jennifer. She'd had a long day, and it was only two thirds of the way over. The shock that registered on her pretty face when Cynthia told her the money had paid off a past due note at the bank just about broke his heart. There were two reasons he couldn't go stay with his parents. He hated to admit it, but one of them was that Jennifer was here.

"I'll try not to bother you." *Liar.* The familiar crush feelings that he'd felt years ago had come rushing back the moment he'd entered the barn. Even in oversize coveralls, Jennifer's presence red-alerted all his senses. He'd stood unnoticed, reveling in the view when he should've stepped in before her very feminine footwear gave out.

Jennifer paced with her hands in the front pockets of her jeans. What was she thinking?

"My room is on the opposite end of the house. The only time you'll see me is mealtime and maybe some evenings."

She stopped pacing right in front of him. "Why'd you pick our ranch for your dig?" Jennifer rubbed her lips together.

Brett shrugged. Lying wasn't his style, but would she want to know the truth?

Jennifer's blue eyes bore into his, trying to extract an answer from him. Sadly, if he kept eye contact, they probably would. Brett looked away and cleared his throat.

Excited about receiving a grant, planning to fund a dig

abroad, he'd called his parents to share his news. After they congratulated him, they'd brought him up to date on his hometown. They'd heard Matthew Edwards was having a little bank trouble. Wasn't he always gracious about letting Brett bring kids to his property to dig holes? Weren't the bluffs on his land similar to the ones where the bones of Sue T-Rex were discovered? Wouldn't leasing the land help Matthew and be a win-win for both of them? Subtlety wasn't his parents' long suit.

"You knew?"

Brett lifted his eyes to hers. He was certain this information would not improve her day. He nodded and hoped the silent reply would suffice.

Jennifer scrubbed her face with her hands.

Don't cry. Don't cry. Don't cry.

At least Cynthia was here to handle the tears. Women were better at this type of thing. Brett looked over to the stool but no Cynthia. He looked around. When had she slipped out of the room?

"Faith is a small town...." Brett stopped in the middle of his lame but truthful excuse when Jennifer parted her hands and gave him a "you're a dead man" look.

"Don't you dare say you rescued me." Jennifer's voice shook but there were no tears in her eyes.

"Jennifer, if Matthew hadn't suffered a stroke you wouldn't even know about this, so this time I'm not rescuing you."

Jennifer dropped her hands and her eyes grew wide.

"That didn't come out right. All I was trying to say was you'd still be in Chicago enjoying your life." Brett stopped talking when her eyes grew wider.

"My life." Jennifer's ragged intake of breath emphasized the silence in the room. "I'm up for a promotion, but I haven't even called my boss." Jennifer rubbed her lips together and ran her fingers through her hair. The short chestnut strands softly falling back into place.

"I'm sure she'll approve your time off."

The look Jennifer gave him screamed doubt. His attempts at helping weren't working.

"I don't think I can keep my promise to Dad." Jennifer's blue eyes, draped in sadness, focused on him. "I don't think I can stay and run the ranch."

All the surprises of the day were starting to set in. Would it help to embrace her?

Jennifer slid back onto a stool and rested her chin in her hand. "Everything has changed so much. How can I do this?"

"You helped your dad run the ranch for years. You can do this." Brett walked over to Jennifer and rested a hand on her shoulder, giving it a squeeze. "Nothing's really changed."

"I know nothing about bison." Jennifer stared into space.

"Eldon does. Listen to him. You'll learn."

"Like he'll teach me. He thinks I'm too citified." She shrugged his hand from her shoulder. "But judging from the laughter earlier in the barn, he's not the only one."

Brett tucked his hands into the front pockets of his jeans. Searing fingers of heat crawled up his face. He'd laughed for the joy of seeing her again, not because of Eldon's comment. He liked those heels. Even now he was having a hard time keeping his happiness at being near her again from showing on his face.

"I think Eldon needed to be mad at something because of the tense situation. He chose your shoes. Men do that."

Jennifer considered his explanation for a few moments.

"I'm sorry I laughed," he said. "It wasn't really directed at you. Just guy stuff. Bad excuse, I know. I came out of the barn to apologize, but that's not how it ended up. I guess we have too much baggage from our youth."

"That's the reason you shouldn't stay here. Please go to your parents' house."

"I can't. It breaks the contract." He wished that Jennifer would let this drop.

"If I know Dad, your agreement was a handshake, not a contract. So I don't really see why this is such a big deal." Jennifer raised her palms in the air.

"You're partially right. Our contract is a handshake. However, one of the qualifications of the grant requires that I stay on the dig site. If the grant committee found out I wasn't staying on the dig site, they could pull the grant."

"Which means?"

"They'd shut down the dig and demand the grant money back. Like your dad, I've already spent the money, not to mention I have archeology students who'd be without coursework. Whether you want to or not, Jennifer, we're sharing a house for a few weeks."

Jennifer rested her chin on her hands. Her shoulders sagged.

"There's something else. Every summer I host a two-week dig for inner-city kids. They'll be staying here, too."

Jennifer shook her head and stood up. "Cynthia told me." She started toward the hallway that led to the two bedrooms on the opposite side of the house from where Brett's room was located. She stopped in the hallway door and half turned. "I can't see any way that any of this will work out." Then she disappeared around the doorway.

Her defeated body language and features turned Brett's heart to mush. If there was ever a time Jennifer needed to be rescued, it was now.

Chapter 3

Jennifer entered the bedroom of her youth. Even the familiar comfort of her teenage sanctuary didn't ease the dread in the pit of her stomach.

She walked to her bedroom window, the one where she'd wished on stars and tried to visualize a world filled with skyscrapers and traffic noise.

She needed to call her boss at *Transitions* to extend her vacation, though she was certain that would affect her promotion to beauty editor. Maybe she'd put off making the call until all of her dad's tests were back and a plan was in place for his rehabilitation. The doctor thought they'd have the test results back today and be able to determine the severity of the stroke.

"You okay?" Cynthia carried a basket full of bedding into the room. "Thought I'd get your bed freshened up for you."

Jennifer hadn't even noticed the lack of bedding on her canopy bed.

"So that's where you disappeared to."

Cynthia smiled. "You and Brett had business to discuss that didn't involve me."

"Like everyone in this area doesn't know everyone else's business." Another thing Jennifer didn't miss about ranch life and small-town living.

"Still, didn't involve me." Cynthia waved a fitted sheet through the air and it settled across the double bed. She tucked a corner of the mattress into the pocket closest to her.

Jennifer moved to the opposite corner and repeated Cynthia's motions. "Do you think the financial stress of the ranch caused Dad's stroke?"

"No, Matthew doesn't worry about money. He never has. I'd guess his cigar smoking contributed." Cynthia tucked the corner of the mattress into the sheet and waited for Jennifer to finish her side.

"He hasn't started smoking them again, has he?"

Cynthia whipped the top sheet through the air. It snapped then floated down to the bed. "No." Cynthia laughed. "You hammered him hard on that issue when you were a teenager, telling him you didn't want to be an orphan. He threw an almost full box of cigars into a bonfire. I've never seen anyone quit cold turkey like that before. But after thirty-plus years of smoking them, I'm sure they did some damage."

"Thanks for getting him medical assistance so fast. The hospital told me it could have been worse." Jennifer tucked the flat sheet under the mattress.

"We were lucky. It happened during breakfast. Brett knew what to do. He's a good man."

How many more times was Cynthia going to tell her that? Jennifer exaggerated a sigh. "I'll have to thank him."

"That's long overdue, I think." Cynthia lifted the basket. "I'm putting fresh towels in the main bathroom. Nothing's changed here. Supper's at six. Better not put off your phone call. The business day is almost over."

Between Cynthia's hints and Brett's presence, this was going to be the longest few weeks of her life. Jennifer looked around the room. The cordless phone still sat in its cradle. She lifted it, punching the on button to check for a dial tone. She pressed in the number and waited for the connection.

Jennifer splayed her free hand in front of her. Her three-day-old French manicure looked pretty good.

"*Transitions,* how may I direct your call?"

"Jacque Gleason, please." Jennifer switched hands and continued to inspect her manicure.

"Jacque here."

"Hi, Jacque, it's Jennifer."

"How's your dad?"

Jennifer sat on the edge of her bed. "He only suffered one stroke. They're still running tests to make sure there are no other blockages. Then they'll determine the course of his rehabilitation."

"Sounds like the doctors are on top of things."

"Yeah." With all that had happened, it was difficult for Jennifer to sound hopeful.

"Are you staying close to the hospital?"

That had been Jennifer's plan when she left Chicago. "No, I'm at the ranch. I went straight to the hospital when I got here, but Dad made me promise to help run the ranch while he's in the hospital. So here I am. In fact, that's why I'm calling. I'll probably need to use my two weeks of vacation time. He should be home by then."

"You think so?" Jacque's voice didn't sound too sure.

"I guess. The doctors thought he'd be released to a

rehabilitation facility in three days. I'd think with three weeks of intense therapy, he'd be ready to come home."

"Have you talked to the doctor about that? I went through this with my mom, so I've learned not to assume too much. It depends on the severity of the stroke. It takes some stroke victims months to recover, and then—" Jacque stopped midsentence and cleared her throat "—they may not ever be one hundred percent. Jennifer, have you considered that?"

"Yes." Tears burned Jennifer's eyes. Once the numb fog of shock from seeing her dad's distorted features wore off, it was all she'd thought about on the long drive to the ranch. Even if Dad couldn't run the ranch, he wouldn't want to leave his home. Even though she no longer called the ranch home, she understood why he'd want to stay here. She'd come up with a plan to hire an in-home caregiver, but knowing the ranch's current financial state, that might not be an option. The situation left her feeling helpless.

"I don't think your two-week vacation is going to cover the time off you need for this situation." Jacque's voice slipped from a friendly, caring tone to all business.

Jennifer massaged the bridge of her nose. "Can I use FMLA?"

"You can. It's unpaid though."

Closing her eyes, Jennifer tried to remember the balance in her savings account. It might cover half a month's rent. Considering the ranch's financial state, she couldn't borrow any money from her dad.

"I know you need to stay and help your dad, but we still need to put out a magazine. You can do your job from there."

Handling the duties of her upcoming position as beauty editor at an off-site location would be tough enough but mixed with ranching responsibilities, it seemed impossible. "I don't know."

"Do you have internet access there?"

"Dad doesn't have it, but I'm sure it's possible."

"Check into getting it. You can email me your beauty and advice columns. Simone will mail the beauty products the office receives for review to you on a weekly basis. If you can't get internet access, we can work out mailing deadlines, but I really hate to go that route."

Beauty and advice column? "Does this mean I lost my promotion to beauty editor?" She applied more pressure to her fingertip massage, trying to alleviate the pain of an impending stress headache. She'd worked very hard at her job and deserved the promotion, yet right now all she wanted was some time off to help her dad deal with his health issues.

"It means—" Jacque sighed "—I'll have the intern who was taking over your columns fill in during the summer months. We'll revisit the editor position when things settle down for you."

Jennifer exhaled louder than she'd meant to. The events of the day were overwhelming. She needed some free time to absorb all that was happening but didn't have the energy to reason with Jacque.

"Jennifer." Jacque's voice softened. "I'm trying to help. I know you need to be there for your dad, but we need you, too. Helen's retirement from beauty editor left us shorthanded. If you take FMLA there's no one to cover the beauty sections of the magazine. Are you willing to try my suggestion?"

No, she wasn't, but what choice did she have? Promotion or not, she couldn't quit; she still had rent and utilities to pay on her apartment in Chicago. "Yes," she whispered into the receiver before pressing the disconnect button.

* * *

The smell of yeast tickled Jennifer's nose, arousing her from her nap. A pang of hunger shot through her. The quick salad she'd grabbed in the mall, combined with the taxing activity of pulling the calf, had left her ravenous. She arose. She reached for the ceiling and her aching arm muscles and back protested with pinpricks of soreness. She stretched deeper before relaxing her arms.

Turning, she found her suitcase and purse sitting right inside the doorway. How nice of Cynthia!

She rummaged through her purse for her makeup bag and hurried into the bathroom to freshen up for supper. Based on the smell of the bread, it was close to being ready.

"Do you need any help?" Jennifer entered the kitchen, leaned against the island counter and watched Cynthia pull dinner rolls from the oven.

"It's under control." Cynthia brushed the crusty tops of the rolls with melted butter.

"What are we having? It smells wonderful." Jennifer inhaled.

Cynthia smiled. "Your favorite, Tater Tot casserole."

"Yum." Jennifer took the basket of rolls Cynthia held out, carried them to the red-and-silver Formica kitchen table. She'd begged her Dad to update the kitchen furniture during her teenage years. Now she knew people in the city that paid high prices to furnish their homes with retro chrome tables and chairs.

"Thank you for carrying in my suitcase and purse. I appreciate it."

"You're welcome."

Brett's deep baritone startled her and Jennifer's body jerked.

"Sorry, I wasn't trying to sneak up on you, but then

again, I am wearing sneakers." Brett pointed to his footwear and snickered.

Cynthia chuckled.

"Don't encourage him." Jennifer rolled her eyes in mock disapproval. "That's a lame joke." Brett had changed into black athletic pants and a white T-shirt that stretched across his broad shoulders. He wore his dark hair longer now. Combed straight back, the waves turned into curls that brushed the back of his neck.

"I know." Brett winked. "But the kids will love it when they get here."

Jennifer smiled. "They sure will. The staff at the magazine is always trying to come up with wordplay jokes, aimed at girls' interests, of course."

"Did you call your boss?" Cynthia looked up from filling four glasses with milk.

"Yeah." Jennifer sighed.

"Is the time off a problem?" Cynthia slid two glasses toward Jennifer and the other two toward Brett.

"Yes and no." Jennifer set the glasses beside two of the place settings on the table. "They asked me to continue my columnist position and expect me to work from here."

"You say that like it's a bad thing." Brett's face showed genuine concern.

Jennifer shrugged. "It is to me. I was in line for a promotion to beauty editor. I was supposed to start that position on May first.

"You can ask to be put on family medical leave." Brett placed the two glasses he carried beside the remaining places at the table.

"I did, but it's unpaid and the magazine is shorthanded. They're depending on me the same way that Dad is. Can we get internet access out here?" Jennifer looked from Brett to Cynthia and forced a smile.

Cynthia pointed to Brett. "He does."

"At least that isn't a problem."

"We have a problem?" Eldon came through the mud porch into the kitchen rolling down his long sleeves and re-snapping the cuffs of his plaid Western shirt.

"Jennifer needs internet access because her boss wants her to work from here while Matthew recuperates." Cynthia slipped oven mitts over her hands.

"Oh." Eldon didn't disguise the doubt on his face or in his voice. He pulled out a chrome frame chair with a red-and-silver padded seat covers and sat down at the head of the table.

"Take a seat." Cynthia motioned to the table with a nod of her head and set the casserole in the middle of the table.

When everyone was seated, Eldon cleared his throat. "Brett, it's your turn to say grace, unless you'd like to, Jennifer."

"I would, if Brett doesn't mind." She turned to Brett.

"Be my guest." Clasping his hands, he bowed his head.

It'd been a long time since Jennifer had said grace, but she needed something from God. "Lord, bless this food that we are about to receive. Let it nourish our bodies the way Your word nourishes our souls. Please keep a healing hand on Dad's body and spirit. Lord, I'm not up to the tasks that have been laid before me. Following in your servant Gideon's footsteps, if this is Your will, I need a sign. Amen."

Jennifer lifted her head and opened her eyes while the others murmured, "Amen." She noticed Brett had pulled his brows together, creating a deep crevice at the bridge of his nose.

Brett unclasped his hands and turned his gaze to Jennifer. His expression held more than a trace of disbelief. Did he think she wasn't a believer?

Before she could defend herself, and her beliefs, Cynthia stood. "Since this is too hot to pass, hold up your plates and I'll serve."

Brett held his plate close to the baking pan.

Eldon grabbed two rolls, passing the basket to Jennifer. "I checked the calf before I came in. You'd never know there was a difficult birth. It's taking nourishment from its mom. Sorry if I was a little hard on you today, Jennifer."

Jennifer caught the two men exchanging a brief look as she buttered her roll. Had Brett mentioned to Eldon what she'd said this afternoon? Probably; he always did meddle in her business.

"What are you going to name it?" She held her plate up while Cynthia scooped a serving of Tater Tot casserole on to it.

"This one's yours to name. We had three more cows give birth today. Several of the buffalo cows appear to be ready to drop anytime." Eldon sipped his milk.

"Do they ever have trouble during the birthing process the way that cattle do?" Jennifer took a bite and savored the tasty casserole.

"Nope, never. I'm going back to check on them this evening. You'd better come along."

"Sure. Cynthia, you have outdone yourself on this casserole. I don't ever remember it tasting so good."

"Thank you. I do make it a little differently now."

"Do you add a different spice?" Jennifer scooped up a big bite. "Mmm…" She closed her eyes.

"Not a spice, an ingredient."

Jennifer opened her eyes. "A different brand of Tater Tots?"

Cynthia shook her head. "I use bison instead of beef."

"Really." Jennifer's gaze fell to her plate. When she lifted her eyes, she realized everyone had stopped eating and was watching her reaction. She forked another bite. "I guess I know why Dad is raising them. They are delicious."

She swore she heard a collective sigh of relief.

"Am I still on my own for breakfast?" Jennifer asked before taking a sip of milk. That was the only meal her dad had ever cooked, thanks to Cynthia. She'd insisted that Matthew needed to start out his day with his daughter in his own home, especially when school was in session. Otherwise Cynthia fixed their meals.

"If you are asking if Eldon and I still eat breakfast at home, the answer is yes. However, you aren't on your own." Cynthia smiled at Brett.

"You don't have to worry about me. I can fix my own breakfast." Brett held up his plate and Cynthia scooped more casserole on to it.

"Did you eat breakfast with Dad?"

Brett buttered another roll. "Yes, we took turns cooking."

"I'll take you up on your offer." Jennifer didn't really want to start her day staring across the breakfast table at Brett, but she'd promised her dad she'd run the ranch, and this was the way their ranch ran. "We'll take turns."

"Okay." Brett shrugged. "I'll take tomorrow."

Jennifer dabbed her mouth with her napkin. "I'll take over Dad's chores."

"Will you be able to do that and your job at the magazine?" Cynthia asked, beginning to clear plates.

"I guess we'll see."

"Might as well start now." Eldon pushed his chair away from the table. "Let's go check on the buffalo."

"Cynthia, you want help with the dishes?"

"No, go on and check the livestock."

* * *

Jennifer sat in the middle of the bench pickup seat, knees to her chin, so Eldon could shift.

"You'd have more leg room if you angle your feet over here." Brett slid a little closer to the passenger door, allowing extra room on the floorboard for Jennifer's feet.

You could have stayed at the ranch house. "I'm fine." Jennifer tucked her boots closer to the cushioned seat.

Brett flashed a doubtful look her way.

"Really, I am." But she wasn't. His spicy cologne drifted her way. They kept bumping shoulders when the pickup bounced through ruts in the rough dirt road to the west pasture.

"Are buffalo hard to raise?"

Eldon downshifted before he drove through a huge pothole left by the winter snowfall. "Not really. You have to make sure the fences are high so they can't jump over, but other than that they pretty much take care of themselves. They are the original free-range animal."

She heard the pride in Eldon's voice. Native Americans held the buffalo in high regard.

Eldon rounded a corner of the pasture, and the shaggy-coated bison came into view.

"How many head do we run?"

"About fifty." Eldon looped the pickup around three trees to point in the direction they'd come from.

"The kids got a big kick out of seeing them last year." Brett smiled. "Matthew pinned one and let them stick their hands through the fence to pet it. They were awestruck."

Eldon laughed. "Those kids are awestruck about everything to do with the ranch. Remember the little boy that was amazed by the lights in the sky. He'd never seen the stars before. Imagine that." Eldon shook his head in disbelief and slipped out of the pickup cab.

Brett held the passenger door open until Jennifer was standing beside him, then he pushed it shut with a quiet click.

"Are they skittish?" Jennifer looked out at the buffalo grazing on round hay bales.

"Not usually, but you never know."

The first rule of ranching included being on alert around the animals. Let something spook one, and you could get hurt.

Eldon made his way toward the herd with Jennifer following close behind.

Brett kept pace beside Jennifer, stepping high like he was marching in a parade rather than walking through a pasture.

"I wish I'd put my boots on," he muttered.

"What's that?" Jennifer pretended she hadn't heard his complaint.

"Nothing." He kept his eyes to the ground.

Jennifer grinned, planning to tease Brett when she ran smack into Eldon's back. She grasped his arm to recover her balance.

"Sorry. What is it? Is one in trouble?"

Eldon stood transfixed. She stepped to his side, trying to follow his line of vision. She saw two bison calves suckling on their mother. "Eldon?"

He lifted his arm and pointed.

A small black nose surrounded by white wooly fur peeked under its mother's middle.

Jennifer squinted. "Did a buffalo adopt a beef calf?"

"I don't think so." Eldon strode in front of Jennifer. "It just can't be." He looped around the fenced edge of the pasture to view another angle of the newborn. Jennifer and Brett followed.

"It's not?" Brett asked. He no longer marched through

the short grass, but walked briskly until he reached Eldon's side.

"It is," Eldon said, stopping short. He removed his cowboy hat. "It's a miracle."

"What is it?" Jennifer squared her shoulders and pushed between the two men.

Brett let out a low whistle. "I think it's your sign."

Chapter 4

A white bison calf, a sacred sign in the Native American culture, suckled nourishment from its mama. Jennifer froze, mouth gaping. Growing up around the Lakota people, she knew their beliefs. They believed they were witnessing a miracle in this newborn calf.

"I'm going to get a closer look." Eldon stepped around Jennifer, walking slowly toward the grazing herd.

The low chant of Eldon's native prayers drifted through the pasture, snapping Jennifer out of her mesmerized state of mind.

She turned her head toward Brett. "I can hardly believe my eyes. I'm going to get a closer look, too." She took a step.

Brett's firm grasp on her arm halted her. "Jennifer." Brett's deep baritone was a low whisper. "I think Eldon needs to be alone right now. Let's go call Cynthia. We can wait by the pickup until she arrives."

"I've got my phone." Jennifer kept her voice low while reaching inside her blue jean jacket for her phone.

"You won't get a signal out here. We'll have to use the radio in the pickup." His grip remained firm on her arm. He pulled her in the direction of the vehicle.

Jennifer stumbled over the uneven ground. Pulling her arm free, she stopped to regain her balance. She'd fallen once today and didn't plan on an encore performance. Brett turned. She took a forward step, flicking her wrists so her hands waved up and down, shooing him toward the pickup.

The swish of her denim boot-cut jeans mixed with the crunch of grass under Brett's exaggerated steps seemed amplified in the quiet countryside. When was the last time she'd noticed subtle sounds? The noise of a living, breathing city drowned out the rustle of clothing or click of a stiletto on the sidewalk.

Jennifer sighed. Chicago. That's where she should be. But then again… She glanced over her shoulder to glimpse the white calf. She watched Eldon's figure turn shadowy in the fading daylight while Brett called Cynthia on the CB radio in the truck.

"Do you really think the white calf is the answer to my prayer?" Jennifer asked as she approached the pickup, keeping her voice low.

Brett eased the tailgate of the pickup down so the click and clank of moving metal wouldn't frighten the herd. Palm out, he gestured for Jennifer to sit down. She slipped onto the tailgate, letting her legs dangle over the edge. Brett sat. The makeshift bench momentarily tilted when he rested his weight sideways on the edge, one leg dangling, the other touching the ground.

"Maybe. God does send us signs all the time. Most of us are too busy to notice them."

Another dig at her lifestyle. Irritation pushed the wonder of seeing the rare white buffalo from Jennifer's mind.

"Nothing has changed. You'll do anything to spoil my moment." Jennifer crossed her arms with an indignant huff.

"Your moment?" Brett drew his brows in confusion—mock confusion.

"I'm tired of everyone making remarks about my career choice. If you haven't noticed, I've had an emotionally stressful day. Seeing this white calf gave me hope that if I keep my promise to dad, run the ranch until he's better, then everything else will turn out okay."

"Oooooh." Brett drew the vowel out. His eyes widened, giving Jennifer the impression that he hadn't been pretending, that he was truly confused. "By turn out okay, you really mean keeping your promotion?"

"No." Jennifer's retort echoed through the quiet. Where was the white noise of the city when she needed it? She cleared her throat before lowering her voice. "I mean that *everything* turns out okay. Dad gets better. The ranch becomes solvent. The kids have a good time and, yes, I keep the promotion."

Jennifer turned. Stretching her neck she looked back at the pasture. Emotional exhaustion nudged out the exhilaration at first seeing the white buffalo calf. Her shoulders sagged. Could this really be the answer to her prayer? Her sign from God? She turned back to Brett expecting to see his mocking grin; instead, she found his face somber.

She squirmed under his intent stare. Jennifer cleared the shame from her throat and met his gaze. "I believe I misunderstood your answer."

The corner of Brett's mouth twisted up, not quite into his mocking grin. "Yeah, I got that."

Jennifer broke eye contact, staring into the darkening horizon.

"Apology accepted."

Defensiveness surged through Jennifer. She looked from the vast nothingness back to Brett. "I didn't…"

His cocked eyebrow and full smile stopped her indignant response.

He knew how to push her buttons. Always had. His smile faded, but he never broke eye contact. She slid her hands down the stiff denim of her pant legs, gingerly resting them on her bruised knees. Her stomach twisted. His deep brown eyes seemed to bore into her, scrutinizing her the same way they had when they were growing up. She couldn't keep the agreement he had with her dad. She looked away.

A few moments ago, she'd thought she'd found the answer to her prayer; now responsibilities tensed her shoulders.

Brett scooted across the tailgate, their legs a mere inch apart. He placed his hand on her shoulder. "Just have some faith, Jennifer. Everything will turn out okay."

The gesture and the tenderness in his voice were a comfort, yet his touch sparked emotions she hadn't dealt with in a decade. Fighting the urge to cover his hand with hers, she jerked her shoulder free of his grasp.

The purr of the approaching ATV's motor overpowered nature's night sounds and muffled Brett's indignant snort. He slipped off the tailgate.

"Now that Cynthia's here, I'll take you back to the ranch. You've had a hard day. You need some rest."

Brett stopped in front of Jennifer, facing her. He blocked any chance she'd have of moving. "I know the answer you want to hear is that the buffalo calf—" Brett pointed toward the pasture "—is the answer to your prayer. I know that to the Native American people, a white buffalo calf is a sign. What I don't know is if it's your sign."

Last night it had taken all of Brett's strength to watch Jennifer wilt like a flower after a hard frost at his inability to agree with her about the newborn calf being her sign. He wanted to circle her in a tight embrace, assuring her that she had people to depend on to help her through this rough time.

Brett looked down at the coffee filter, unsure of the number of scoops he'd poured in it. He dragged the measuring spoon through the grounds adding one more scoop. Judging by the pad of soft footsteps around the house last night he knew that she hadn't slept much, either, so high-octane coffee would be a necessity today.

Once he started the coffee brewing, he tried to quietly prepare breakfast. He'd heard Jennifer pacing through the house until after two this morning. He would let her sleep a little later, but running a ranch did require early hours.

Brett's stomach gurgled louder than the coffeemaker finishing its brew cycle.

Pouring a cup of java, Brett watched the water in the saucepan come to a boil. Matthew begrudgingly ate oatmeal. Brett hoped Jennifer didn't share that gene because today it was oatmeal. He stirred the oats into the boiling water. Placing the lid on the pan, he removed it from the heat.

He rubbed his tired eyes. Matthew's diet had contributed to his stroke. He ate unhealthy frozen breakfast entrees because they were quick and easy, ignoring the trans fats that contributed to his high cholesterol. At least after Brett moved in Matthew had prepared fresh food for breakfast when it was his turn to cook. Although eggs fried in bacon grease were still far from healthy.

The squeak of door hinges followed by footsteps cut through the silent house.

"Good morning." Jennifer rounded the island counter and reached into the cupboard for a coffee cup.

A light, clean fragrance, reminiscent of sheets dried on a clothesline, wafted through the air when she walked past him. He breathed deeply.

"Good morning."

"What's for breakfast?" Jennifer lifted the lid of the pan. "Hmm…oatmeal."

"You don't take after your dad in that department." Brett smiled. "Excuse me." He pointed to the cupboard behind Jennifer. "I need to get the toppings."

"Toppings?" Jennifer giggled. "We're eating oatmeal, not an ice cream sundae."

"A spoonful of sugar helps the oatmeal go dooowwwn," Brett sang out the familiar film tune.

Jennifer laughed. "Practicing for the kids again?"

"Guess you could say that." Brett shrugged. "Although most of my sugar is the natural type—" He set several containers filled with dried fruits and nuts on the counter. He rummaged through another cupboard before he pulled out a package of brown sugar. "I do cheat a little bit."

Jennifer sipped her coffee. Her eyes rounded. "I know why you're so peppy now. This is stronger than most espresso."

"Sorry, I lost track of how much coffee I added to the filter. Guess I shouldn't have put the last scoop in. Should I make a different pot?" Brett said, placing two steaming bowls of oatmeal on the counter.

"No, I can drink it. Besides, I'll need it. I didn't sleep

very well." She sighed. "Too much on my mind." She
slipped onto a stool.

"Do we need anything else?"

Jennifer surveyed the items spread out before her.
"Milk. I pour milk over my oatmeal."

Brett retrieved the milk from the refrigerator and slid
onto a stool. "Shall we say grace?"

Folding her hands, Jennifer gave a quick nod while
swallowing her sip of coffee.

"Lord, thank you for the nourishment to strengthen our
bodies. Bless our efforts as we go about our work today.
Help us handle anything unexpected with grace. Amen."

Jennifer said amen but narrowed her eyes and furrowed
her brow at him. No doubt thinking the last part of that
prayer was odd. With everything that had happened yesterday, he knew her brain was overloaded. She wanted
to believe the birth of the white buffalo calf was the answer to her prayer. Last night his mind had replayed the
situation over and over, always coming back to the same
ending: the unusual birth would complicate the running
of the ranch.

A companionable silence filled the kitchen. Jennifer
shook dried cranberries and walnuts onto her oatmeal,
topping it off with several spoonfuls of brown sugar before pouring milk over it all.

Her fashionable hairstyle showed off her dainty ears.
Triangles of silver and turquoise dangled from her lobes.
Her long-sleeved chambray shirt was buttoned to the neck
but untucked, shirttails grazing her hips. A turquoise
neckerchief was tied over the collar of her shirt. It was
a holdover from her youth; while other girls sunbathed,
Jennifer covered up her ivory skin to avoid sunburn. He
had his mother to thank for that.

Jennifer caught him drinking in her nearness. She

pursed her lips. "Your oatmeal is getting cold." Her tone turned from friendly to gruff.

Yet another holdover from their past. Any time Jennifer caught Brett appreciating her beauty, she became agitated. Brett sprinkled a teaspoon of brown sugar over his oatmeal before adding blueberries and almonds.

Of course she still covered up her beauty with makeup. Although he had to admit that she'd toned down her makeup quite a bit since high school. She'd lost her heavy hand and vibrant red colors. Now her face looked dewy, more natural. Staying out of the sun had also paid off for her; other than the tiniest of smile lines by her eyes, Jennifer had no signs of aging.

His own deep sigh echoed through the kitchen, snapping him out of his dreamy thoughts and into the present. Jennifer gazed at the refrigerator, her mouth puckered, her jaw set. Brett looked down at his untouched oatmeal. He scooped his spoon through it.

What was he doing? He was no longer a love-starved pup. She'd always made it crystal clear to him that she didn't want his affections. Why had he thought it would change now? Besides, she preferred the city's skylines over the vastness of the open plains, a preference he would never share. He kept his eyes on his bowl, watching the mound of oatmeal disappear with each spoonful. He needed to keep his focus on his dig and his research.

"Good morning." Cynthia burst through the door ahead of Eldon.

"Morning." Brett and Jennifer mumbled halfhearted greetings at the same time.

Cynthia stood on the opposite side of the counter, eyebrow cocked, alternately staring from one to the other. Then she harrumphed before turning to pour herself and Eldon cups of coffee.

"Guess Eldon and I are the only ones excited about the miracle that happened on the ranch."

Eldon pecked a kiss on her cheek when she handed him his cup of coffee. "Are you going to tell them or should I?"

"What? Is something wrong?" Jennifer dropped her spoon.

Brett pushed his oatmeal bowl a few inches back on the breakfast bar's counter. He lifted his cup, sipping his coffee. The bitter brew washed away the dried fruit's sweetness. Maybe it was a good thing he'd brewed strong coffee; Jennifer was going to need it. He knew nothing was wrong. Cynthia and Eldon's beaming smiles should have alerted Jennifer to that fact. He should have prepared her for this news, instead of staring at her like she was a priceless piece of art.

"Nothing is wrong." Cynthia chuckled.

"Then what is it?" Jennifer retrieved her spoon and lifted a bit of oatmeal to her lips.

"We just got off the phone with the tribal elders. The group should be here later today to begin prayer ceremonies."

The chink of the spoon hitting the Formica countertop resounded through the kitchen. Brett caught it before it fell to the floor. He stuck it in his bowl.

"A prayer ceremony." Jennifer began to rub her temples. "What will that involve?"

The irritation in Jennifer's voice wiped the smiles from Cynthia and Eldon's faces.

"We'll move the buffalo to a pasture that is easily accessible. Many elders from different tribes will come. They will determine how long the ceremony takes. It could be days. We'll know more when they get here."

"I don't need more to do. I have chores, calling the doctor, setting up a home office, calling dad, getting housing ready for the kids."

Cynthia engulfed Jennifer's hand with her own to stop her from physically counting her to-do items off on her fingers. Eldon's low growl stopped her.

"You won't have to do anything." Eldon set his cup on the counter with enough force that coffee sloshed over the edge. "Did the city lights burn the importance of this birth from your memory? Don't begrudge us our faith."

Brett saw the anger building in Eldon. He held up his hands palms out. "Hey, hey, hey. Give Jennifer a break, the past twenty-four hours have thrown quite a few things at her."

Another low growl filled the kitchen; this time it came from Jennifer and seemed directed at him. "I suppose you think you're rescuing me again." Her words snapped out.

In an instant her eyes widened and her features registered regret. He knew he'd received the brunt of her frustration. But that didn't stop a small thread of hurt from stitching his heart.

"I think—" Cynthia's calm tones broke through the tension filled kitchen "—that Brett is right." She nodded toward Brett before shooting pointed looks to Eldon, then Jennifer.

Brett pushed himself off the stool. Feeling it teeter, he caught it before it fell. He gathered his breakfast dishes and took them to the sink. Arms braced on the metal sink, he stared out the window at the rocky bluffs that outlined the Edwards ranch. Why did the only girl he ever cared deeply about refuse to let him help her, love her?

"Jennifer, we know you feel overwhelmed, but this birth is very important to our culture. You wouldn't want to interfere with our beliefs, would you?" Cynthia's soothing voice quieted the room.

Brett turned in time to see Jennifer drop her eyes and shake her head. The urge to rescue her was so strong. He swung his arms behind him and then gripped the stainless steel molding of the sink so tight that he thought his fingers might leave dents in the surface.

Moisture blurred Jennifer's blue eyes when she lifted her head. "I'm sorry, it's just too much. I never wanted to…" Her voice trailed off when Eldon cleared his throat.

They could all finish that sentence: run the ranch. Brett wanted to make suggestions. Solve her problems. Rescue her. He knew she didn't want that. He needed to walk out of the kitchen right now. Go out to the dig site. Let the Clearwaters and Jennifer figure this out. But his heart wouldn't let him.

"The only disturbance for you will be the coming and going of vehicles past the house. Someone else will take care of everything that revolves around the white buffalo." Cynthia broke into a wide smile. "That is part of our excitement."

Brett's nutritious oatmeal turned into a heavy lump of dread that fell to the pit of his stomach. *Someone.* In all his rehashing of the repercussions of the birth of a white bison calf, he hadn't even thought of *someone.* There was only one someone who would puff out both Cynthia and Eldon's chests with pride. There was only one someone who had now settled down and was involved in his Native heritage. There was only one someone who had a bond with Jennifer so tight that no one could break it.

"Lance is coming out to the ranch to stay and handle all matters that pertain to the white buffalo calf, including media." Cynthia's excitement raised the pitch of her voice until he thought she'd squeal at the end of her statement like a teenage girl seeing a heartthrob.

Brett swallowed hard, twice. Once to swallow his less-than-thrilled-with-this-news grunt, the other to clear the bitter taste that lingered on his tongue, not from the strong coffee, but the jealousy that the mention of Lance Clearwater's name evoked.

Chapter 5

It took two weeks, and a lot of patience on Cynthia's part, but Jennifer finally mastered centering the hayfork into the round bale, lifting it and maneuvering the tractor to the appropriate pasture. Yesterday after her first successful loading and delivery of the hay, she'd been so excited that she had called her dad. He'd laughed at her exuberance, filling her heart with joy.

The May weather coaxed shoots of green from the ground. Soon the land would supply their cattle and bison nourishment on its own, and she'd cross off one of her daily chores.

As the tractor bounced through the rough ground of the pasture to the road access, diesel fumes tickled her nose, reminding her of the delivery and garbage trucks on the streets of Chicago. A sudden breeze wafted the acrid scent of manure through the air. Grinning, Jennifer decided diesel was the only scent the city and the country shared.

Jennifer chugged along the gravel road toward the ranch house. The flat land allowed easy visibility to the bluffs that pushed up through their land like stalagmites in a cave—which was the main reason Brett had wanted to befriend her in their youth. He loved the open land, and the secrets that it held.

Squinting into the sun, she scanned the bottom of the jagged crags. The golden rays reflected off something white: tents. She'd found Brett's dig site. She slowed the tractor and considered making a visit to their resident professor.

Professor. Her smile widened thinking of Brett in his professional manner. Movement on the face of a bluff caught her eye and she saw several people standing there. Although she'd never seen them, they must be the graduate students he'd mentioned on her first night at the ranch. One waved frantically toward the tent. The distance mixed with the sputter of the tractor's motor weren't conducive for eavesdropping but the silent motion picture reeling before her said they'd found something.

A form emerged, the breeze flapping the loose sleeves of a white gauze shirt. Brett hurried toward the group, hopping up on flat levels of rock with the same skill a professional mountain climber might use to scale the lower ridges. When he reached them, he bent down studying the earth. Had his group uncovered another prehistoric find? Another Sue T-Rex? If so, there would be no living with Indy.

With no break in the fence line to allow tractor access in this area of the ranch, Jennifer continued to watch the scene play out. After a few minutes, Brett stood, patted another person's back and skittered down the rock's side to the white tent below.

Curiosity piqued, Jennifer decided that she'd pay a visit

to the dig site. She pushed on the gas, braced her body to absorb the shock of the bouncy ride and steered for home. She turned into the back entrance of the ranch to avoid any traffic jams in the main lane. Eldon had moved the white bison calf to a pasture closer to the highway, where the passersby might catch a glimpse of it, the gathering crowd would have easier access and no one would disturb her or Brett's work.

She maneuvered the tractor to its designated spot in the machine shed. The engine coughed. The behemoth shuddered when she switched the key to Off. Jennifer peered down at the metal step and considered using it to dismount. Instead, she jumped from the edge to the concrete floor. The impact of her boots on the cement jarred her body. Next time she'd dismount the tractor the right way.

That teenage action had always irritated her dad. *You'll break your neck.* Recalling his warning she began to smile, but then the reality of his current health crisis hit her. Sadness tugged at her smile and heart. Although his speech was coming back, every evening when she called him she still carried the conversation. She planned to visit him this week, but his insistence that the two-hundred-mile round trip could wait until calving was over came through loud and clear.

A comforting lilt of prayers drifted through the air. Jennifer leaned against the wide opening of the machine shed, watching the ceremony taking place down the knoll from the building.

Onlookers surrounded the fencing, while the Lakota people prayed. Tribal members from California were scheduled to arrive. The drum and harmonizing voices, expressions of their faith, reminded her of her neglect to commune with her God. She closed her eyes, and though she was still uncertain that the white bison was her sign, she whispered, "Thank you, Lord, for the good report from the doctor. Although Dad requires rehabilitation, he will recover. Praise be to you! Please help his recovery to be speedy and successful."

"Amen."

Jennifer's body jerked.

"Sorry, I didn't mean tō startle you."

A tall figure approached her from behind and stood beside her, blocking the warmth of the spring sun.

Jennifer turned to look at her childhood friend Lance. He'd changed in the same way Brett had: muscles replaced sinewy arms, shoulders widened, a boy turned into a man. He wore his black hair short and gelled into place instead of long.

"Lost in thought." Jennifer shrugged.

"I believe you meant lost in prayer." Lance wrapped an arm around Jennifer's shoulder, pulling her into a tight side hug. "I'm sorry about Matthew."

"Thanks, me, too. I call him every day but…"

"It's not the same as being there. I stopped by the hospital before driving out here. He told me that you've called. He hears the worry in your voice. He says stop."

Jennifer quirked an eyebrow at Lance before she returned his hug and resumed leaning in the door opening, this time facing him.

"I know. Parents. They always worry about their children, but the children should never return the emotion." She pulled off her leather gloves, whacking them against the building. The snap emphasized her frustration.

Lance shook his head and grinned. Jennifer giggled. They'd been each other's allies and sounding boards about their parents for so long the subject could still easily erase the years.

"I was able to set up the rehabilitation over the phone.

He's adamant that I stay out here and oversee the ranch. Something your dad is much better at. I think I'd do more good in Rapid City."

"Maybe, maybe not. Peace of mind can help a person heal." Lance shifted his weight from one foot to the other, rocking his body. "It's been a long time. The city is treating you well. You've never looked better." Sincerity flashed through Lance's brown eyes.

"Thank you."

"Are you still mad at me?"

Jennifer peered in the direction of the harmonious voices, even though the elders were no longer in sight. Lance, her best friend, had hurt her. Then that hurt had turned to anger. She'd thought she was over it, but his question stoked the smoldering coals of the past, causing a spark of old emotion to flame up inside her. Dragging her eyes from the horizon, she stared back into his. "Are you apologizing?"

His face scrunched before he let out a loud peal of laughter. "You can't be serious. That was years ago. No one got hurt."

That wasn't true; she had. Her best friend had betrayed her. *Thank God Brett had been there or I wouldn't be living my dream.* Realization squeaked from her throat. Someone else had gotten hurt, too. "You didn't get hurt, but others did."

Lance slipped his hands in his jeans pockets and shrugged. "Everything worked out fine."

"That doesn't mean that you don't owe me," *and Brett,* "an apology."

His eye-roll response threw gas onto her spark of anger. The flames exploded inside of her. Tilting her head, she studied her friend. More than ten years later, he still refused to take responsibility for his actions. She turned and walked away. The sound of her boots slapping against the cement floor of the machine shed bounced off the metal walls of the building.

"Hey, aren't you going to answer my question?" Lance's voice echoed through the open rafters.

"Yes, I'm still mad at you." Jennifer shouted her response, her words crackling through the building like dry wood in a bonfire. She marched out of the side door of the machine shed without turning back to look at the person who had once been her best friend.

A glance at the microwave dampened Jennifer's spirits. She didn't have time to travel out to Brett's dig site. Her conference call to the office started in fifteen minutes. Snagging a cookie bar from the container on the counter, Jennifer headed to the small bedroom in the front of the house that her dad had converted into an office.

She'd rearranged some of her dad's items to accommodate her laptop. She was still without her own internet access. Brett loaned her his Wi-Fi device when she needed to respond to an email using her laptop. Opening up a document, so she could jot down notes from the meeting, Jennifer finished her midafternoon treat and picked up the handset of a black phone.

Taking a few deep breaths, she tried to release her irritation about her job situation. She should be in Chicago, preparing the intern to take over the beauty column at *Transitions*. Instead, the intern was adding valuable editor experience to her resume. Jennifer's heart clenched. She knew that she was where she needed to be, but after six years of hard work at the magazine, it didn't seem fair.

Jennifer dialed the number. She splayed the fingers of her free hand out. Manicures were no match for ranch work, even when protected with leather gloves. Whether she liked it or not, the polish needed to be removed. She'd have to give herself a manicure, something she hadn't done in a long time. She sighed, missing her nail salon appointments.

Once the call got under way, Jennifer focused on the magazine themes for October and November. She loved every aspect of putting together the magazine. Although she couldn't see the layouts, Jacque described them the best she could. Any pictures pertaining to the beauty column would be emailed to Jennifer for approval.

When the call ended, Jennifer had good notes on what her upcoming columns would include. She hit Save on the document at the same time a light rap sounded on the door jamb.

"I thought you were in here. Did you need to use my internet?" Brett entered the room with the small device in his hand.

"No, this was a planning session." Jennifer swiveled in the antique office chair that matched the rolltop desk.

Brett stood behind her. "What does evergreen topic mean?"

Jennifer frowned and folded her laptop screen down. Leave it to Brett to stick his nose in her business. Ready to retort, she remembered her curiosity about his dig site this morning. This might be a chance for her to explain her work, help someone to understand its importance.

She motioned for him to sit down in a straight-backed chair beside the oak desk. "An evergreen topic is advice that can be covered every year, through every season." Judging by Brett's expression, that wasn't a good explanation.

"In the summer, I always have a column about the benefits of wearing sunscreen at the beach or pool. A winter topic is caring for chapped lips."

Brett nodded his understanding. "Don't your subscribers get bored, seeing the same topics every year?"

"No, the evergreen topics are rotated on a three-year basis, then I always change the advice based on new research in the industry. Plus, our magazine is for tweens, which is a short age span, so the chances of our subscribers reading the same evergreen topic are minimal."

"I see." Brett rubbed his chin. "So what are you writing about for your evergreen topic this summer?"

Jennifer picked up a copy of a magazine. "I wrote about caring for your hair in heat and humidity." She pointed to bold red words on the front of the magazine. "Magazines publishing schedules are six months ahead of the calendar year. The column I'm working on now is for the October issue."

"So what's the evergreen topic?"

"I'm thinking about something to tie in to the harvest, maybe moisturizing for the upcoming winter months." It felt good to talk shop. She knew her voice reflected her excitement about the subject.

"Do you ever miss writing something more meaningful?"

"What?" Hurt bubbled up in her chest. This was not the direction she'd thought the conversation would go. Same old Brett, he'd seemed interested in hearing about her work but really he wanted to insult her interest in makeup, beauty and fashion.

"Writing a beauty column *is* meaningful, and important." Jennifer spat out the words.

"That's not what I meant." Brett raised his voice in defense.

Jennifer adjusted the volume of her voice to match his. "There are lots of little girls..."

"Brett, I sent you to find Jennifer, not argue with her."

"Mrs. Lange!" Jennifer jumped from her chair and embraced the stylish woman. "I didn't know you were here."

Jennifer followed Mrs. Lange's disgusted glare.

Brett's posture sagged. "My mom's here to see you."

"And I'm staying for dinner so we can catch up. You look terrific, Jennifer." Mrs. Lange stepped back admiring her.

"I owe it all to you, Mrs. Lange." Jennifer loved Brett's mother. Most ranch women dressed like Cynthia, in jeans and T-shirts. They saved dress clothes and makeup for special occasions. Not Mrs. Lange; she wore impeccable makeup and trendy clothes all the time. She'd taught Jennifer how to apply everything from foundation to eyeliner so it would enhance her features.

"Please call me Marilyn. You're a grownup now." She waved her arm, jangling the bracelets around her wrist. "I love the color of lipstick you're wearing."

"Thank you. I might have an unused tube of it if you'd like to try the color." Jennifer hoped Marilyn would try it. Her makeup color palette was outdated.

Out of the corner of her eye, Jennifer saw Brett stand. Walking behind his mother, he lifted his eyes heavenward. "I'll find Cynthia and let her know she's not on kitchen duty tonight, since you brought all of Jennifer's favorites."

Jennifer wanted to roll her eyes, too, at his jealousy of her relationship with his mom.

"Sure, if you have an extra, I'll try it." Marilyn jerked her head toward the door. "I'd better go with him to make sure everything gets put away properly. It'll give you time to freshen up." Marilyn winked at Jennifer before following her son from the room.

Lifting her shirtsleeve, Jennifer sniffed. Diesel fumes lingered on her clothes. She hurried to her room to change. Jennifer hummed while she freshened up for her afternoon visitor. Even though she had a few outdoor chores to finish after dinner, she donned one of the dresses she'd packed when she'd thought her stay would be a short vacation. The wraparound dress's red-orange hues accented the highlights in her hair. She slipped into low-heeled sandals; the straps matched the colors in her dress.

Using a lighter hand than if she was in the city preparing for dinner, Jennifer applied her makeup. Gliding a rust-colored lipstick over her lips, she surveyed her image in the mirror of her vanity.

Perfect.

Brett's heart flipped when Jennifer entered the room. Her dress skimmed her body yet flounced when she moved, playing hide-and-seek with her feminine curves. Multicolored hoop earrings grazed her shoulders and framed her "made up for a night on the town" face.

Although it was applied tactfully, it was still too... He struggled with the right word. His eyes rested on her lips. Bright. He preferred her subtle everyday look. She didn't need layers of makeup to be beautiful. She was naturally gorgeous.

Brett looked at his mom, all dolled up, with red rosy cheeks and eye shadow covering her eyelids to the arch in her brows, in a color that had gone out of style when he was in grade school. He remembered how she'd taught Jennifer how to apply makeup. Had she encouraged Jennifer to be heavy-handed again today after he left the room?

A low whistle cut into Brett's thoughts. Turning he saw its source and his chest tightened.

Lance Clearwater sauntered into the living room, brushing against a pedestal lamp on his way to Jennifer.

The lamp swayed. Brett caught it before it fell, never taking his eyes off of Lance, who wasn't taking his eyes off of Jennifer. A burning sensation started in the center of Brett's gut as he righted the lamp.

"You always did clean up good."

At this angle, Brett couldn't see Lance's face, but he imagined an appreciative glow shone from his eyes by the way a blush crept up Jennifer's neck, spreading to her already too red cheeks.

"Thank you." Jennifer's wide smile and fluttering eyelashes moved the fiery ball of jealousy from his gut to his chest. It squeezed around his heart. When he looked at Jennifer with respect and appreciation, all he received in return were glowering looks.

A disgusted huff filled the room. His mother's wide-eyed stare snapped him back to the present. He cleared his throat. "Excuse me, I have a tickle in my throat. Must be lingering dust from the dig site."

His mother's tight smile indicated his excuse was lame.

Lance turned. "Still playing in the dirt, Lange?" He chuckled and plopped down into a chair.

"He's a professor of archeology at the School of Mines." Jennifer sat down beside Brett's mother. "But you probably already know that living in Rapid City." She turned from Lance to his mother. "You must be so proud of him."

"We certainly are. *Although...*"

His mom dragged the vowels out in the word. Brett knew what was coming. "Mom." She turned her head at his command.

She shrugged, turning back to Jennifer. "So sue me, I want a grandchild. I'm sure Matthew does, too." She rested her hand on Jennifer's arm. "Is there a special someone in Chicago?"

Every nerve in Brett's body bolted to attention. Busy giving in to his feelings about Jennifer, he'd never considered that she might be dating someone in Chicago.

Jennifer shook her head. "No."

"I bet you date a lot though." His mother smiled sweetly at Jennifer. The same sweet smile she used when she wanted to extract information.

"Not really." Jennifer rubbed her lips together. Her nervous tell. His mother's line of questioning obviously made her uncomfortable.

"Mother, it's none of your business." Brett crossed his arms to reinforce the sternness of his voice. His mother never looked his way.

"Why not? I've known her forever. Pretty girls…"

"You mean knock-out," Lance interrupted, looking directly at Brett with a smug smile.

Brett fought to control the fierce jealousy threatening to overtake him with Lance's goading. It was hard, but the Bible said to turn the other cheek. Brett would have to trust God to even the score between him and Lance. He'd done the right thing, rescuing Jennifer that night. He took a deep breath. Right now he needed to do it again. Only this time he needed to save her from his mom's nosey questions.

"Would anyone care for something to drink? We have sun tea, lemonade or soda."

"Oh my." Jennifer stood. "Where are my manners? Let me get the refreshments."

Once everyone made their choice, Jennifer hurried to the kitchen. She needed to get away for a minute and compose herself. Marilyn and Lance had both caught her off guard. She loved her heart-to-heart talks with Marilyn, but in private. She hoped no one noticed her tight smile or the tears of hurt brimming in her eyes that she'd tried to blink back at Lance's insincere compliment. Jennifer pulled a serving tray from the cubby in the kitchen island.

"Sorry about that." Brett stepped through the doorway to the refrigerator. He pulled out a sun tea jar decorated with yellow and orange butterflies.

Jennifer lifted glasses from the cupboard. "You have nothing to apologize for." She held a glass under the ice dispenser of the refrigerator. The machine groaned as it released the ice cubes.

Brett rolled his eyes. "Yes, I do. My mom's questions are out of line."

"Not really." Jennifer smiled and handed an ice-filled glass to Brett. "Your mom and I have had more intimate conversations than that."

Time and space turned to slow motion. The glass began to slip from Brett's grasp. The astonishment on his face turned to panic as he tried to regain his grip on the glass. Jennifer started to snicker.

Brett caught the glass before it hit the floor. He frowned at her so she tried to suppress her merriment but ended up releasing it in small coughs of giggles. Soon a belly laugh bounced out of Jennifer before she could stop it.

"The look on your face is…" More guffaws choked out her words. She handed the other glass to Brett before she dropped it and hung on to the counter for support. Unable to control this giggling fit, she gave in to it. Her eyes moistened, releasing a tear that trickled down the side of her face.

Through water-filled eyes, she watched Brett shake his head, then begin to laugh.

"I don't think it was that funny." He crossed his eyes at her, causing another round of laughter to bubble out.

"I'm sorry." Jennifer sucked in a breath, trying to control her glee.

"Don't be. You need to laugh more." Brett's expression softened, his brown eyes filling with sincerity.

"I don't have much to laugh at these days."

Brett's brow creased. "That's not true."

A tingle of aggravation wiggled through Jennifer. No one else seemed to see the enormity of the responsibilities in her situation.

"So you had heart-to-heart talks with my mom?" Brett wrinkled his nose.

"You act like you had no idea."

"I didn't." Brett reached for the two empty glasses to fill them with ice. Pushing the glass under the dispenser, the ice tinkled against the metal before clinking down into the glass.

"What did you think we talked about when your mom shooed you out of the house?"

Brett shrugged. "Makeup. You both seem enamored with it."

The tension she'd released through laughter snaked back through her shoulders. She placed her hands on her hips. "What is that supposed to mean?"

"Nothing." Brett filled the glasses with tea.

"Don't give me that. I've never forgotten how you told me I wore too much makeup growing up."

"I was a kid." Brett turned; when their eyes met, she saw that same judgmental scrutiny.

"I still see how you judge me when you look at me." Jennifer flipped her hand through the air.

"What?" Brett's baritone rose to the pitch of a tenor.

"You heard me. What's wrong with a little makeup?" Jennifer planted her fisted hands on her hips.

"Nothing's wrong with a little makeup, but you don't plan your life around it."

Jennifer felt her eyes widen. She was tired of everyone's wisecracks about her occupation. "This coming from a man who plays in the dirt for a living."

She saw anger flicker through his eyes. Angry embers had been smoldering since Lance had made his wisecrack a few minutes earlier.

She removed one glass of tea from the tray and set it on the counter. Putting the pan of chocolate chip bars in its place, she huffed out of the room.

Chapter 6

It wasn't Brett's turn to cook breakfast, but he shoved the baking pan filled with cinnamon-laced, egg-soaked bread into the oven. He had risen extra early this morning. Jennifer had managed to avoid him at breakfast for the last week. Not that she skipped her turn providing breakfast— a bowl filled with dry cereal waited for him on the counter each morning. Sometimes, she was out doing chores; other times, he heard faint noises coming from the office.

He was guilty of ducking her right after their argument, too. He tried to understand their differences. He'd been trying to for years. He just didn't get it. The dig site provided the excuse he needed to avoid Jennifer. The graduate students uncovered a few arrowheads and dish fragments. Buzzing with excitement over their finds, they kept excavating until dusk made it difficult to see to dig. By the time Brett returned to the ranch house, the other occupant had called it a night.

He poured a cup of coffee. Turning off the dim light under the stove fan, he crept into the living room and slid into the leather recliner. The overstuffed chair creaked under his weight. He stopped all movement. He felt bad that he'd planned this ambush, but he wasn't taking any chances of missing Jennifer this morning. They needed to talk.

He inhaled the hazelnut aroma before sipping the nutty brew. He rested his head against the high chair back and waited. The first light of day filtered through the blinds, brightening the room and casting shadows through the house.

He finished his cup of coffee at the same time a faint beeping came from down the hall. A muffled noise, like the thud of a cell phone on the floor, followed. A door creaked opened. He expected to hear the muffled noise of Jennifer's morning routine; instead, she padded into the living room, stretching her arms in an arch over her head.

"Good morning."

It started as a squeak, then gradually rose an octave to a shrill shriek that seemed to last five minutes. Brett scrunched his shoulders, half expecting the window glass to shatter.

Jennifer ran into the kitchen and flipped on the light switch before he could get out of the chair.

By the time he made it into the kitchen, Jennifer was pacing back and forth in front of the kitchen island. "I didn't mean to scare you." Why did he always mess things up with her? Yes, he'd wanted to make sure they were able to talk, but he hadn't planned on startling her. He figured she'd see him in the dim light of the room.

"What are you doing up?" Jennifer puffed out the words. Her breath came fast and uneven. She clutched her chest.

Brett didn't answer, couldn't answer. He was too busy trying to control his own rapid heartbeat. Under the stark brightness of the kitchen lighting stood the most beautiful woman he'd ever laid eyes on. Her flawless ivory skin, tinged with pink over her cheekbones, took his breath away. Her long eyelashes fluttered as she adjusted to the bright lighting. Her tousled hair invited him to run his fingers through it to comb it back into shape.

In two steps he closed the gap between them and lifted his fingers, but before he could touch her hair, her eyes widened and her mouth gaped. She closed her eyes, raising her palms to cover her bare face.

"Don't." Brett gently covered her hands with his pulling them away from her face. "You are so beautiful." His whispered compliment ate up the silence of the kitchen.

He braced for her angry response when her eyes searched his.

Instead, she smoothed her hand through her hair, dropped her arms to her side and looked away.

Grazing the silky skin of her cheeks with his fingertips, Brett leaned down. "Look at me."

Trepidation filled Jennifer's blue eyes when she did as he'd asked. She rubbed her lips together. Her nervous habit drew his eyes to her pressure-darkened lips, lips that invited Brett to discover their softness again. He'd dreamed of that kiss, reliving the moment, his reward for her rescue.

The jackhammer rhythm of his heart made it hard to breathe. He leaned in, aware of Jennifer's ragged intake of breath. He lifted his eyes to hers. Emotion pooled in her eyes to a depth he'd never seen before. This was the real Jennifer, not the girl who hid behind makeup and fashion trends. The realization spurred him into action.

He brushed his nose against the tip of hers. In seconds, he'd feel the sweetness of his dreams.

Beep, beep, beep. In unison, they both started. The relentless oven timer continued to sound.

Jennifer's hand pushed on Brett's shoulders. "One of us needs to get that before it burns." Her voice, thick with emotion, sounded slightly lower than normal.

He searched her face for a trace of…something. Disappointment? Longing? The desire to kiss him? What he found was an apologetic look.

She shrugged before slipping past him. "With the ranch's finances, we can't afford to let food burn."

The beeping stopped. Brett drew a deep breath, suddenly aware of the cinnamon aroma in the kitchen.

"I thought it was my turn to make breakfast."

Brett turned as Jennifer slipped oven mitts over her hands, opened the oven door and bent down.

"I thought we needed to call a truce."

When Jennifer stood, red flamed her cheeks. Not sure if the heat of the oven caused the crimson color or if she was still angry, Brett babbled on. "We need to talk. The kids will be here in two weeks and we have to get ready for them. So we need to discuss sleeping arrangements, meals…" Brett's voice trailed off. Jennifer leaned against the counter shaking her head.

Did that mean she wasn't ready to lay aside her anger?

"How did that sneak up on me? I have a hay field that needs to be cut. My column deadline is tomorrow, and I still have the beauty tip to write and two responses to readers' letters. I didn't even consider the meals. Will Cynthia need help preparing them?"

"I don't think so. She didn't last year, but I did create a menu for her." Brett reached into the cupboard for plates. "This is what I thought we could discuss over breakfast."

Jennifer gingerly lifted a hot piece of French toast from the baking pan and dropped it on a plate. "I can't, not this morning. I have to get the rough draft of my column finished before I go out to check on the food and water situation with the white buffalo. Plus it's a good idea to keep track of who is on the ranch. We're expecting more media today. The public television station should arrive sometime this morning."

The beautiful blue eyes Brett had stared into moments ago now glazed over in deep thought as she reviewed her to-do list.

"Then I need to haul water to the west pasture. I hope to drop by your dig site today. But first, I have to write that column. They usually just write themselves." Jennifer managed to cover her French toast with powdered sugar and pour coffee while ticking off all of her chores. "I can't figure out why I'm having so much trouble."

Brett knew why; she had too much on her mind. It seemed he'd vanished into thin air. Jennifer might be talking, but it wasn't to him.

He cleared his throat to remind her of his presence. "You need to sit down and eat your breakfast. We don't have to make plans. Maybe sitting still *and relaxing* will help your creativity."

She sighed. "Thanks, but I really can't. Maybe by late afternoon, I can get out to the rocky crag to check out what you and your students are up to. We can talk then." Jennifer padded out of the kitchen, still ticking off items on her to-do list.

He'd thought she'd been avoiding him, but in reality, she was stretched so thin that her days started at sun-up, maybe before. Brett mentally wrote an item on his to-do list. Talk to Eldon. Jennifer needed help—if he had to pay for a hired hand, he would.

* * *

Dark clouds banked up in the western sky. Jennifer paused, holding the screen door half open. Today might not be the best day to travel out to the bluffs that ran down the middle of the western section of her father's ranch. She jingled the ATV key in her hand and rubbed her lips together. She turned, re-entering the house.

"I thought you were going out to see Brett." Cynthia carried a basket of folded towels out of the laundry room.

"I'm going out to see the dig site that is on my father's property," Jennifer clarified Cynthia's statement, then returned the ATV key to a hook on the wall before removing the pickup key. "Rain clouds are forming to the west so I decided to take the pickup. I need to stay here and work, but I told Brett that I'd stop by this afternoon."

Cynthia set the basket on the counter. She smiled at Jennifer. Removing the dish towels from the basket, she placed them in a drawer. "Good, you two are on speaking terms again. Will you both be joining Eldon and me for dinner now?"

"What?" Jennifer crossed her arms and cocked at eyebrow. "I've eaten dinner with you."

"On and off for about a week, just like Brett. Seems to me when you join us, Brett doesn't. When Brett joins us, you don't."

Under Cynthia's point-blank stare, Jennifer lowered her arms. There was no intimidating this woman. "I'm sure we'll both be joining you tonight." Jennifer had planned to eat in the office so she could pay the bills. Guess this meant she'd be pushing her bedtime back an hour or two.

"I need to get going. Brett wants to talk about the kids' food and lodging."

"Mind if I ride with you? I'm anxious to see those arrowheads Brett's crew uncovered." Cynthia rubbed her palms together.

"I don't mind at all. I wonder if the graduate students have determined the age of the arrowheads. They could easily be manufactured tourist trinkets."

"Maybe—" Cynthia shrugged "—but how would souvenirs get clear out there? The land does border the Cheyenne River Reservation."

"True." Jennifer slid behind the wheel. Once they fastened their seat belts, she eased the pickup down the lane. Vehicles lined both sides of the long driveway. Vans, campers and tents dotted some of the pasture.

"How long will this last?" Jennifer peered over the steering wheel to the fence where the white bison rested beside its mother.

"As long as the bison lives. The white buffalo is an important sign of well-being on the verge of an awakening in traditional Native American beliefs." Cynthia lifted her hand in greeting to a group of people.

Peacefulness embraced Jennifer. Maybe the white bison was her sign, although the well-being of the ranch and her promotion still eluded her. She frowned and eased the pickup onto the highway.

A short quarter of a mile later, the pickup tires bounced over the washed-out gravel road that led to the bluffs. The vehicle rolled through deep ruts that caused the steering wheel to vibrate Jennifer's arms worse than the construction workers' jackhammers' tremors on Chicago's downtown sidewalks.

"This road needs a little grading." Jennifer fought to keep her teeth from clicking together.

Cynthia held on to the arm rest. "Not a priority. We only work on a priority level. Brett's group are the only ones who use this road."

Soon, the road ended, and Jennifer drove along the fence line across the rocky pasture. She parked beside another pickup with an over-the-cab camper.

Both women descended from the truck and walked to the tented area a few feet away.

Long tables lined the edges of the tent. Desk lamps and microscopes were interspersed with odd-looking tools. A young man, clad in magnifying glasses, sat at a table carefully removing dirt from something with a brush, while Brett watched over his shoulder.

"Is that an arrowhead?"

Brett turned and smiled. His brown irises were enlarged by the glasses he wore. "It's not, but there are some in that box over there. One's in very good condition."

He slipped off his glasses and walked over to Jennifer. "I'm glad you took a break and came out this afternoon." He held his hand in the direction that Cynthia walked. "You should take a look at what we found."

"Is it the Holy Grail?" Jennifer kept her tone light, raising her eyebrows in innocence.

Brett laughed. "No, nor is it the Ark of the Covenant." He teased back. "These are objects that show the history of the land you own."

They walked over to where Cynthia stood. Jennifer peered into the case. Fragments of pottery and several small arrowheads lay on soft fabric.

"Think there was a Lakota village here at one time?" Jennifer twisted her head to see the objects at different angles.

"Could have been. Or some warriors passing through. That is what this type of dig is all about. We're hoping to unearth other items that might give us a clearer picture."

"Is this where the kids will dig too?"

"No, they'll be farther over, by the shale rock. I'm hoping they find some fossils."

The tickle of a thrill shot through Jennifer. Not because of what was being found on their land but because Brett's work linked the past to the present and Brett made it sound interesting.

"Are they safe out here?" Cynthia nodded toward the treasures in the box.

"Yes, but I do need to get them back to the school so they can be cleaned and analyzed. I'm probably going to make a trip to Rapid City tomorrow or the next day."

"Great. If I make a shopping list, will you pick up the extra items we need for the kids' dig?" Cynthia asked.

The kids. That was what Jennifer had come out to discuss. She'd been so engrossed listening to Brett talk about his work, the topic had slipped her mind. "Is that all we need to figure out?" Jennifer looked from Brett to Cynthia.

"No, we need to work out sleeping arrangements, daily schedules and other activities besides learning about the dig."

"I guess we'd better get started." Jennifer started to walk to a chair.

Cynthia placed her hand on Jennifer's arm to stop her. "I have a better idea. I'll make up the shopping list tonight. You ride with Brett to Rapid City and visit your dad. Use the one-hundred-mile trip to plan for the inner-city children."

"I'd love to see Dad, but I have too much work to do. I can't spare a day to go to Rapid City." Jennifer flipped her hands in the air.

"What is more important—work or visiting your father?" Cynthia crossed her arms over her chest. Her eyes dared Jennifer to say anything. Respect for elders in the Native culture was a number-one priority.

"Maybe we should see if it's all right with Brett. He might not want to tag along."

Jennifer hoped that Brett saw the pleading in her eyes. After all, she'd shared her list of tasks in this morning's conversation.

"It's fine with me."

Obviously, Brett couldn't read pleading or he was afraid of Cynthia, whose stance and expression grew sterner.

Jennifer sighed. "I guess one day wouldn't put me too far behind."

Brett wrinkled his face. "I guess it might not work. I need to stay overnight. I set up a meeting with another professor for Friday midmorning."

Relief washed through Jennifer. She wouldn't get behind in her chores, after all. "I guess that settles it. I'm staying at the ranch."

She turned toward Cynthia, who now added a headshake to her stance. "If memory serves, Rapid City has several hotels."

She'd lost the battle with Cynthia. Jennifer waited in her dad's suite at the respite care facility while the physical therapist took her dad to a rehabilitation session.

The suite was a large square. The small living room area, with a matching love seat and wingback chair, was decorated with plastic-framed prints of seascapes. A flat-screen television hung on the wall that separated the rooms. The bedroom held a standard hospital bed with a small accordion-door closet. The handicap-accessible bathroom was large and roomy.

"Back already?" Jennifer closed her laptop and placed

it on the unoccupied cushion of the love seat in her father's room.

Her dad stopped pushing the walker. He tried to open his arms wide. The left arm cooperated, but his right arm hung loose in midair. He motioned more with his left hand than his right for her to come over for a hug.

Closing the short span of space between them, she wrapped her arms around her dad, burying her face in his neck. The familiar smell of Old Spice pulled her back to her childhood, when all he had to do was hug her to solve her problems. Unexpected tears sprang to her eyes. She missed this. She missed him.

His comforting embrace tightened on the left side, his left hand firm on her shoulder while his hand brushed her waist on the right. "My girl. I've missed you."

Jennifer sniffed. "I've missed you, too." She pulled away. Hands on his shoulders, she studied his features. His age was showing. The shallow crinkles around his eyes were now deep crevices. His hairline had gone from receding to nonexistent; a few tufts of white hair speckled his scalp. The stroke hadn't affected his features or dimmed the twinkle in his blue eyes.

"How are you feeling?" Jennifer stood to the side.

The metal walker jangled. Her dad threw more than moved his right hand to the walker's grip. He stepped forward with his left foot, then slid his right foot up to meet it. "Never good after that therapy session."

As she watched his slow progress to the chair, Jennifer's heart ached for her father.

"But, if I want my former life back, I have to put up with it. Oomph." He dropped into the chair, his breath an audible pant.

Her aching heart sagged at his statement. Would he be able to recover his full mobility? They were lucky the stroke hadn't affected his speech much. He slurred a few letter pronunciations but could still talk.

"Tell me how the ranch is doing." Matthew moved the walker to the side of the chair with his good hand.

Jennifer reclaimed the cushion on the love seat. "Pretty good." She tried to inflect happiness in the tone of her voice since she was lying. After balancing the bank statement, pretty bad was more accurate.

Her father's bull snort echoed through the room. "You're either pretending because of my health or Brett dug up buried treasure."

"Now, Dad, we don't have to discuss business. I promised I'd take care of everything, and I will. You concentrate on getting better." Jennifer's fingers worried the upholstery piping on the love seat's arm.

"I've put my sweat and blood into that ranch and worried about it all my life. Why stop now? Guess I've missed some excitement. I've heard Eldon's version. Tell me yours."

Jennifer rolled her eyes. "The high heel of my boot broke while pulling a calf, which is not entirely my fault. I didn't know I'd be assisting with that chore when I left Chicago. Eldon..."

Her dad waved his hand, stopping her rant. "I heard the calf lived."

"All the spring calves and cows lived through the birthing process this year." Pleased with the knowledge that no creature was orphaned, Jennifer smiled.

"That is good news. Any more excitement?"

"A white buffalo calf was born. We have Native American visitors from California camping out in our pasture."

"Saw that on the news. Lance's pretty good at drawing media attention to items of this caliber." Her dad's focus was on the black screen of the wall-mounted television.

"Yeah, I guess he is." She pinched the velvety piping between her fingers.

"His scholarship for college sure paid off with a journalism and communications major." Her dad rested his gaze on her.

Jennifer shrugged. "Looks like it." She really didn't want to talk about Lance. She'd been successful at avoiding him.

"Both of your journalism scholarships paid returns. You two probably talk a lot of shop, since you're both in the same field more or less."

Crossing her arms, she raised her brows, letting her dad know that she knew he was fishing for information. "No, we don't really talk much at all."

She watched her father rub his chin while he looked heavenward. When he dropped his gaze, he stared straight into her eyes. "I wonder why that is?"

Jennifer tensed every muscle in her body to avoid squirming under his knowing stare. Or maybe it was a bluff to try to trip her up. "We grew up." She cleared her throat. "*I* grew up and no longer see eye to eye with him."

"Is that so?"

"Yes." She wasn't lying. She knew that Lance owed her, and Brett, an apology for what he'd done.

Her dad grinned, then shrugged. "Have the inner-city kids arrived yet?"

"Not for a couple of weeks. Right after Memorial Day. Brett and I put together a loose plan for activities while they're here."

"Those kids are so much fun. They are in awe of everything—well, maybe not the manure." Matthew's hearty laugh bounced around the room. "None of them are fond of the manure. They love to dig though."

"It surprised me that Brett sponsors a dig for kids."

Jennifer smiled at the joy beaming from her dad's face, making him look twenty years younger.

"I don't know why it would. He's a good person." His expression sobered. "He always was, but you never could see that, could you?"

Her breath popped out of her as if she'd been kicked by a horse. Where had *that* come from? "Dad, he was two years younger than me. I didn't want to be pestered by a lower classman. Now, I guess—" Jennifer jerked her upturned palms in the air "—he's okay."

He's more than okay. Jennifer smiled at her dad, hoping her face didn't reveal her thoughts. Brett had turned out to be quite a handsome man.

"Wait until you see him interact with those kids. It's one corny joke after another."

"I know. He's tried a few out on me."

"I'm sorry that I'll miss that." Wistfulness veiled her dad's face.

Jennifer frowned. "Surely in two weeks…"

"Physical therapist thinks it'll take at least four months here in rehab before I can come home."

This time when life's horse kicked, the pain almost doubled Jennifer over.

Chapter 7

"I can't believe it's going to take four months' rehabilitation." Jennifer flipped the visor down even though the afternoon sky was overcast.

"I think that is pretty good recovery time for a stroke patient." Brett kept both hands on the steering wheel, gripping tightly. Every fiber in his being wanted to flip the visor back up. "It's a blessing that Matthew's speech wasn't affected."

Digging through her massive purse, Jennifer pulled out a small bag. She rummaged through it, lifting and inspecting small plastic cases before resting them on her leg. Jennifer sighed. "That is the only bright spot in this entire situation."

Brett sighed, too. No one needed to apply more makeup to visit Mount Rushmore, especially Jennifer. Although, time had given her a lighter hand with its application and she no longer sported the same "clown cheeks and lips" his mother wore.

Snaps of plastic fasteners, swishes of brushes and sputters of air from squeeze tubes cut through the silence in the car.

"You need to sit back, relax and enjoy the scenery. We're almost to Keystone. When was the last time you visited Mount Rushmore?" Brett momentarily took his eyes off the road to glance at Jennifer.

Her Western-cut light pink blouse complemented her ivory skin. The embroidered flowers across the front and back yokes dressed it up without giving it a big-city feel. Her jean skirt ended right below her knee. The pink strappy sandals added three inches to her height.

She looked his way while rubbing her now muted pink lips together and shrugged.

I'd like to stop that nervous habit of hers with my own lips. Brett widened his eyes. Those types of thoughts kept popping into his mind, since their near kiss yesterday morning. He tightened his grip on the steering wheel, somehow thinking that would help him get a grip on his emotions.

For a few seconds it worked; then Jennifer's lips smacked when she stopped her nervous habit and began to speak.

"I don't know, probably thirteen years ago." She waved a mascara wand through the air. "Maybe fourteen." She strained against the seat belt, until she was inches away from the visor mirror. "Why?"

"It's changed a lot since then. I think you'll be surprised." Brett adjusted his speed for a curve in the highway.

"Changed how? They're presidents' heads carved in stone."

"It's granite."

"I believe granite is stone, *Indy*." She giggled. "I don't know why we didn't stay in Rapid City. I haven't been to Reptile Gardens in *years*." She dragged out the last word.

An involuntary shiver snaked up Brett's back.

"When was the last time that you were there?"

Brett glanced at Jennifer, praying the car ahead of him didn't hit their brakes. Her wide-eyed, innocent expression caused him to arch a brow. She knew the reason they weren't visiting that tourist destination. Even making fun of his weakness, she was a distraction he found hard to resist.

She dropped her makeup products back into the small bag. She lifted a feathery brush and a round container from the bag. After dipping the brush into the powder and tapping it lightly on the side of the container, she swept the brush across her face.

Jennifer laid the brush in the case, zipped the bag and dropped it back into her purse. "Brett."

The abrupt way she said his name brought him out of his hypnotized state. He caught her slight frown before returning his eyes to the road. He slowed as the highway wound through Keystone, consciously making an effort to keep his eyes on the road, not only to avoid hitting a car, but pedestrians, too. This sightseeing trip was the closest thing to a date he'd ever share with Jennifer, so he didn't want to mess it up with a car accident. "What?"

She growled softly, letting him hear her annoyance. She stared out the passenger-side car window at the hotels and tourist shops in Keystone. "I believe you were going to tell me how Mount Rushmore has changed." Her voice now monotone, instead of filled with good-natured teasing.

"Right, well, you can get closer to it now. Although the

Hall of Records still isn't open to the public. There are some walking trails, but the biggest change happens…"

"Oh!" Jennifer clapped her hands together.

"Here." Brett finished his sentence.

The highway wound at just the right angle that the landscape through the windshield was a direct view of the stone images of Presidents Washington, Jefferson, Roosevelt and Lincoln.

"They seem close enough to touch."

"Yet, they are miles away from the highway." Brett grinned at the enthusiasm in Jennifer's voice.

She turned her head to peer from the side window. The road once again curved. Tall thick evergreens swallowed up the incredible carving.

Once inside the state park, they followed the wide cement walkway. A restaurant flanked one side, spewing grill and deep-fryer oil vapors into the air, tempting tourists to stop in for a bite to eat. The space opposite the restaurant housed a gift shop, with merchandise ranging from cheap souvenirs to history books about the various parts of the Black Hills.

The sun-warmed mid-May day, combined with throngs of sightseers, made Brett glad he'd chosen khaki shorts over jeans this morning. "Can I interest you in a treat?" Brett pointed to the sign advertising ice cream cones.

Jennifer shook her head. "You can get one if you want." Her face held awe staring at the Avenue of Flags that lay before them.

Skipping an ice cream treat, Brett followed Jennifer along the cement walkway, enjoying every state's, and some territories', colorful flags. A light breeze lifted the flags' silky fabric, saluting the passing tourists.

"This is wonderful." The wonder in Jennifer's tone matched that of the many visitors around them, whose voices blended together, creating a white noise all its own. Taking a cue from the sightseers, she dug through her bag. "Do you mind taking a picture of me by the South Dakota flag?" She handed Brett her cell phone.

Taking the offered cell phone, Brett nodded, masking his surprise that Jennifer hadn't chosen the Illinois flag. Jennifer struck a pose under the pole. Brett clicked a picture. "Let me get one more." He lifted the cell phone into camera-ready position.

"Would you like me to take a picture of the two of you?" a park employee asked Brett. Brett looked at Jennifer and, taking her shrug for a yes, he handed over the phone.

Joining her underneath the flag, Brett stood a step behind so her right shoulder overlapped his left.

"Stand a little closer together."

Both of them moved a half step toward each other.

"Got it. I'll take one more just in case."

The pine tree's fresh scent mingled with Jennifer's perfume, making Brett feel heady. Or perhaps it was their close proximity. The breeze blew her hair. A few strands tickled his cheek and chin.

"Oops, I have to try again." A tourist, eyes focused on the flags overhead, walked in front of the camera.

Jennifer shifted her weight. Her arm brushed against Brett's, sending tingles up his arm.

"This one's a keeper." The employee held the phone out. Jennifer stepped away from Brett, retrieving her phone. She pressed buttons to view the pictures.

"Thank you." Brett nodded to the park employee.

"You're welcome. You're a very handsome couple. Enjoy your afternoon."

Before either of them could dispute that they were

a couple the employee disappeared into the crowd of tourists.

Happiness jolted through Brett, lighting up his heart. He'd dreamed of being a couple with Jennifer all of his life. Even though it wasn't true, Brett relished the sound of the phrase. Certain that Jennifer wouldn't appreciate being coupled with him and not wanting a simple mistake to sour her mood, he stole a glance her way.

"We're a couple, all right," she muttered. Brett braced.

She held the phone out. "A couple of airheads. We stood under the wrong flag." Jennifer looked at him, flopped her free hand through the air and started to giggle. "Didn't you notice when you took the first picture?"

He shook his head. His focus had been on her. He'd been lucky that he even captured the post with the flags. "Want me to take another one?"

"No." She tucked the phone back into her purse. "This makes a better story."

Brett grinned. "I'd forgotten your saying." He fell into step with Jennifer.

"Hmmm…I stopped saying it about halfway through my senior year. I don't know why it came to mind now. I must be getting nostalgic being home."

Home? He thought home was in Chicago. "Well, you certainly knew what made a good story. After all, you won the school paper's Christmas story contest every year." Slightly turning his torso to avoid bumping into a tourist, Brett's biceps brushed against Jennifer's shoulder. The knit fabric of his polo shirt and the soft cotton of her blouse must have worked like a conductor, judging by the jolt of chemistry that shot up his arm, bringing a smile to his lips and heart.

Jennifer turned her attention to him, and her drawn

brows and wrinkled nose gave her a bewildered look. Had she felt the shock of attraction too?

"You remembered that?" Her pink lips curved into a wide smile. The sun danced on her skin. The tiny sparkles in her makeup that glistened in the light were no match for the twinkle in her eyes.

Disappointed that his touch hadn't caused her puzzled look, his heart sagged a little.

"Sure, you won a coveted box of chocolate-covered cherries every year that you didn't share." He stuck his bottom lip out, in a feigned pout.

Laughter erupted from Jennifer. She swatted at his arm. "Stop that. You didn't need fancy chocolates to celebrate Christmas. Your mother baked Christmas goodies from Thanksgiving right up until Christmas."

"That I shared." Guilt weaved its way through Brett's chest at Jennifer's wistful sigh. Growing up with a mom, he'd taken for granted that all children experienced what he had until he got involved in various organizations in college. Although he was certain that Cynthia baked goodies for Jennifer, it probably wouldn't be the same as your own mother.

Jennifer stopped before the Grandview Terrace. She stepped to the side so they didn't block the path. She turned to face him, shielding her eyes from the sun. "I've never told this to anyone else. I know all the kids thought I devoured the chocolates myself, but I didn't. Do you want to know why I never shared those chocolates?"

A hint of sadness replaced the merriment in her eyes. A lump of emotion that Jennifer would confide in him clogged his throat. He shook his head.

"They were my Christmas gift to my dad. I always wanted to give him a gift that I didn't use his money to purchase. You don't know how relieved I was each year when my name was announced." Jennifer sighed, managing a weak smile. "I'd run into the house and wrap them before he came in from doing chores. I worked on those stories from the start of summer until it was time to submit them to the contest."

Without thinking, Brett pulled her to him, the instinct to shield her from past and present hurts strong. He'd managed to protect her once—would she allow it again? "Well, then all your hard work paid off," he whispered what he hoped were words of comfort.

"I guess."

When Jennifer placed her palms on his chest, he'd thought his embrace might be a mistake. Just as he was about to release his hold, she leaned into him. His heart took control of his body. Its rapid beat drummed through him. His pulse sounded in his ears, drowning out nature's noises and tourist chatter.

Jennifer tilted her head back, searching his face with her soulful blue eyes. His breath quickened. A fleeting thought about her feeling and hearing his heart's emotional response was the last thing he remembered before he dipped his head, his lips descending on hers.

The familiar softness, burned into his memory from a long-ago winter night, soothed the longing for their touch that he'd grown used to living with for all these years. He'd kissed other women, but couldn't sate the yearning for Jennifer. Delight giggled through him when her lips responded to his.

Gentle pressure from her palms on his chest ended the peck of a kiss. The noise of the park increased around him, pulling him out of his emotional state, making him aware of his surroundings. Damp earth mixed with the aroma of grilled food tickled his nose. Happiness heightened his senses.

He searched Jennifer's face. A slight flush gave her a rosy glow. A hint of a smile played on her lips.

He'd kissed her *and* she'd kissed back. In daylight for the entire world to see, instead of under the cloak of darkness. Like last time.

Jennifer's fingers flew over the keys on her laptop, her column almost writing itself. Her thoughts formed her advice in words easy for a young girl to understand. Marilyn, Brett's mom, was the only woman who ever broached subjects with Jennifer that most girls asked their mothers about.

Cynthia had asked her if she had any questions, after their class viewed the "birds and the bees" video at school, but growing up on a ranch, Jennifer understood the basics of making babies. What she never understood was the emotional aspect of all it; that's where Marilyn came in. Although that column in the magazine was handled by a psychologist, Jennifer knew her beauty column helped girls who might not have anyone to turn to for answers to personal questions.

Her column consisted of a short article giving the young girls beauty tips followed by answers to three letters. She reread her copy. She liked it. She'd chosen three fall-appropriate beauty questions, and covered the damage that the cooler wind could do to hair, complexion and lips.

Jennifer lifted a finger to her own lips. Last night she'd relived Brett's kiss in her dreams. A small thrill danced through her. She liked this kiss better than their first one. She rubbed her lips together, savoring the memory of Brett's lips on hers, and wondered how Marilyn would explain the happiness bursting inside her. Puppy love? That was her explanation when Jennifer finally confided that she wanted Brett to stop following her around in high school.

"He has a case of puppy love for you, dear. Who wouldn't? You're the prettiest girl in the county." Marilyn patted her cheeks before wrapping her in a hug that day. When she released her, she said, "You'd better get used to it, too. My son might be the first, but he won't be the last."

Jennifer had dated in college, but it was hard to meet someone in Chicago. It wasn't that people weren't nice, once you got to know them. It was finding places to get to know them.

Was puppy love the reason she was up early and in a good mood? Had the thrill of doing something daring, kissing Brett in public, renewed her energy? Or was it from being in Rapid City? Hearing the hustle and bustle of the city that pulsed through a person's soul, making them feel alive.

Brett had insisted that she drop him off at his condo last night so she could have the vehicle to go back to the respite facility to visit her dad. He'd made arrangements with his colleague to pick him up for his meeting this morning.

Certain her dad wouldn't be ready for a visitor until at least nine o'clock, Jennifer wandered around her spacious room. She'd planned to use this time to work on her column; now that that was done, she didn't know what to do.

Drawing the drapes, Jennifer peered out the window of her fifth-floor room at Hotel Alex Johnson. The freeway buzzed with traffic, but the city streets hadn't come to life. She'd hoped to see—needed to feel, really—the anxious bustle of people commuting to their jobs.

No one knows you don't work here. The thought brought a smile to her lips. She had forty minutes to get ready. She'd hit the streets, joining the masses on their way to work. She knew the experience would differ from Chicago. There'd be no traffic jams or sidewalk crowds to fight, but every downtown burst with excitement during rush hour.

At precisely seven forty-five, Jennifer pushed through the main entrance of the hotel, turning to her right. She slipped on her sunglasses, secured her laptop case over her shoulder and sauntered down the street with determined steps.

If she were in Chicago, her attire would be dressier, with designer labels. Today, she made do with a red paisley sundress with a hanky hemline that brushed her upper calf. A loosely knit black jacket and kitten-heeled black peek-toe pumps rounded out her ensemble. Not the powerhouse image of a corporate leader, but it did scream fledging career girl.

She crossed the street. She'd forgotten about the statues of the presidents that graced the corners in downtown Rapid City. If nothing else, she'd walk past each statue bidding the president good-day. The silly thought brought a smile to her lips. Brett's quirky humor must be rubbing off.

"Good morning." A gentleman, making eye contact, nodded his greeting.

Taken back, Jennifer mumbled hello but doubted the stranger heard her response. Only on rare occasion did a passerby greet you in Chicago.

After walking several blocks and saying good morning many times, and not to bronze statues, Jennifer turned a corner in search of a coffee shop. Her mouth watered for a particular franchise's raspberry white-chocolate scone and rich breakfast brew. She wondered if the barista at the store she visited daily in Chicago missed her. She always seemed happy to see Jennifer walk through the door.

An odd thought struck her when she crossed the street and yet again answered a nod of hello with her friendliest smile. In Chicago, from the time she awoke in the morning until she reached the coffee shop, no one spoke to her, not even other tenants in her building. Maybe the barista only did because her job involved customer service.

Jennifer spied a local shop. As she entered, she breathed in the mingled aromas of cinnamon, vanilla and coffee. A modest line waited to place their orders. People chatted about the weather, and tourist statistics. The line moved forward. She heard the barista greet each customer by name, asking them personal questions about their jobs, their children and their life. She was genuinely interested in her clientele.

Her barista in Chicago said good morning, asked her how she was doing, smiled politely, but it paled in comparison to this. A wave of sadness washed through her. She fought the development of a frown.

"What can I get for you, sweetie?" The lady behind the register offered a big smile to Jennifer.

"Do you have any scones?" Jennifer peered through the closest display case.

"We sure do. Tart cherry or cranberry."

"I'll have a cranberry scone and tall vanilla latte." Jennifer dug into her purse for her wallet.

"Is this to stay or go?"

Jennifer looked around the room. She'd wanted to be a part of the hustle and bustle of Rapid City's business crowd. But standing in line, she realized that she wasn't. "To go."

"Are you here on business or just visiting?" The lady nodded to Jennifer's laptop bag before she pushed the buttons on the cash register.

Jennifer swiped her credit card through the reader.

"Sort of visiting, I guess. I live in Chicago now, but I'm originally from Faith."

"Oh!" The lady clapped her hands together. "I've been to the Fourth of July rodeo. It's a blast. I'm going again this year. Maybe I'll see you there." She ripped the receipt from the cash register. "Thank you for stopping in." Her smile was so genuine compared to the barista's in Chicago that tears threatened Jennifer's eyes.

Jennifer grabbed her breakfast and hurried back to the hotel. Her steps no longer held the confidence of a career girl. Instead of being happy at the friendliness shown to her this morning, her heart hung heavy. How long had she missed this human connection? Been lonely?

How would it feel to walk into an establishment and be greeted every morning by someone who cared enough about their customers to know them by name? Jennifer walked through the entrance to the hotel, only to be acknowledged by the concierge. She straightened her shoulders, determined that when she got back to Chicago, she'd introduce herself to the barista.

Chapter 8

"I think I should have used the other entrance." Brett inched his way up the ranch's main lane.

The small gathering of people had turned into a throng in the two days that Jennifer had been away from home. No, *not home*. Home was her apartment in Chicago.

Several news vans, with large satellites attached to their roofs, parked sporadically around the metal fencing that separated the bison from the onlookers. Additional motor homes dotted the adjoining pasture.

Jennifer rubbed her lips together while massaging her temples. She'd need to add crowd control and litter pickup to her to-do list.

"Your *friend* Lance is doing his job." Brett's emphasis on the word *friend* had nothing to do with their earlier argument, and everything to do with their past.

"I never expected a spectacle of this magnitude." What she'd considered her sign, the birth of the white buffalo calf, was turning into one more burden on her growing stack of responsibilities. She considered praying for another sign. Gideon had asked God for several signs before leading the army. It couldn't hurt. She closed her eyes in silent prayer.

Lord, I need something to show me that everything will work out fine. The white bison is a blessing, yet I'm not sure it's my sign. Please send me another small indication that things will work out for the ranch, Dad and me. Amen.

Parked cars lined their lane up to the long rock formation, which curved around to the house. Brett hit the brakes. Jennifer was propelled forward, her seat belt tightening across her chest. He'd stopped the vehicle with a little too much force, in her opinion. However, this time she kept her opinion to herself, unlike five miles outside of Rapid City when she'd made the remainder of the one-hundred-mile jaunt tension-filled.

Brett had lost the dreamy-eyed look when she didn't share his opinion on what their kiss meant, which resulted in an argument. The silence and tension in the pickup cab made the two-hour trip seem like four, sinking her further into the abyss of her pity party. The cherry on top of her poor-me sundae was the list of items her dad expected to be finished before he returned home in the fall. Now she'd come home to find a massive crowd camped on her land just when she thought she had a handle on her situation.

The old-fashioned screen door flew open. Cynthia ran from the house, greeting them like they'd been gone for weeks, instead of two days.

"How's Matthew?" She wrapped Jennifer in a tight hug. The soft cotton of her T-shirt caressed Jennifer's cheek.

Closing her eyes, Jennifer inhaled deeply, returning

the hug. A bouquet of oregano and basil mixed with Cynthia's soap, a balm to Jennifer's discontent.

It's good to be home.

Jennifer's eyes popped open. She'd thought of Chicago as her home for the past twelve years. A small sprout of the blues that had begun earlier this morning grew. Her melancholy now bloomed in full with that odd thought.

"Are you okay?" Cynthia held her at arm's length. "Is it Matthew?"

"No...well, maybe." She stumbled over her answer, making it a confused mess that matched her own conflicted feelings. How could she explain that the comfort and elation of Brett's kiss mixed with the kindness of strangers soured her mood, rather than lifted her up?

You have an active life in the city, but it's empty. She pushed the thought from her mind. A niggling loneliness embraced her heart.

At least she'd managed to erase the sappy expression Brett wore every time he looked at her since their kiss. She didn't need his visual reminder when she was having enough trouble keeping her own emotions under control. She didn't regret the kiss or the pleasant dinner afterward. But his life was here and hers was in Chicago, and she couldn't encourage Brett's or her own feelings.

"He sounds so good on the phone every morning when I talk to him. Is there something he isn't telling us?" Cynthia placed her fists on her hips. Her tone drew Jennifer out of her brooding thoughts.

Catching Cynthia's hands in hers, Jennifer massaged them with her fingers until Cynthia released the fist, hoping that'd calm Cynthia's unnecessary worry. "The doctor hopes that after four months of rehabilitation, he'll be able to resume his life."

A wide smile replaced the anxiety in Cynthia's features. "That's great news." She sobered and narrowed her eyes, wariness crossing her face. "But you deliver it like it's bad news."

"It is to her." Brett rounded the back of the vehicle, arms filled with plastic grocery bags stuffed with supplies for the kids.

Jennifer didn't miss his snarky tone. The truth of Brett's words, combined with Cynthia's disgruntled expression, made Jennifer wish she could hit the backspace button on the conversation, so she could rewrite her delivery of the news, the way she fixed her columns when she wasn't clearly communicating her point. She drew a deep breath, ready to defend herself from Cynthia's nonverbal reprimand.

"Believe me, I'm relieved that the doctor thinks dad will recover, but—" Jennifer looked from Cynthia to Brett, who stood by the back door of the house "—I need to get back to Chicago...." The same veil of non-understanding dropped over their faces.

"I heard this all the way home." After giving a snort louder than a cinched brahma bull, Brett went into the house, letting the decades-old screen door slam behind him.

Surely they understood she'd never planned on staying long. This was only temporary. Once her dad recovered and they'd chosen any care options he might need, she'd be going back to her life in Chicago.

Jennifer knew she should respect her elders. After all, one of the Ten Commandments was to honor your father and mother, and Cynthia was the closest thing to a mother she had. But this time Jennifer was standing her ground.

"I have a life and career in Chicago." She strove to keep her voice respectful, even though frustrated tears welled in her eyes. "I'm not staying here forever."

"We all know that." Cynthia lowered her eyes, and when she lifted them, her focus was on the horizon in the direction of the white buffalo calf. "An important sign of well-being on the verge of awakening."

Cynthia's words, barely a whisper in the wind, resounded through Jennifer's heart at a megaphone's volume. She felt certain that Cynthia believed the white buffalo was the sign Jennifer had prayed to God to send, and they were all worried for nothing. Were Cynthia's words the answer to the prayer she'd lifted up a few minutes ago?

Squeezing Cynthia's hands in hers, the moisture brimming in Jennifer's eyes wet her lashes. "You're right. We have no reason to worry." Jennifer sniffed. "Dad's well-being is under God's control."

The seconds it took for Cynthia's brown eyes to meet Jennifer's passed in slow motion. "It's true what you said, your dad's fate is in his God's hands."

For the first time in hours, Jennifer started to smile, until Cynthia jerked her hands free from Jennifer's grasp. Shaking her head, she turned on the heel of her boot and marched toward the house.

The squeak of the hinges on the screen door cut through the thick tension between the women. Cynthia stopped; when she turned, her face held no expression, like the tintype pictures from years ago. "Just so we're clear on this, I wasn't talking about Matthew. I was talking about you."

Brett adjusted his fedora, pulling it low in front to shield his eyes from the glare of the setting sun. He marched toward the bunkhouse that sat down a terraced field below the ranch house. A light wind swished the prairie grass in front of him. Judging by its height, Eldon should move a few calves here to fatten them up for fall.

He'd seen Jennifer head this way after the spat with Cynthia. Jennifer's slight frame barely disturbed the grass. Growing up, she'd been taught the art of respecting nature by Eldon, Cynthia and Lance. While he agreed with the indigenous people that they should limit damage, he wasn't taking any chances. The more noise the better. Anything could be lurking under the cover of the grass.

At the thought, Brett picked up his pace, raising his feet higher with each step. He needed to talk, *or kiss,* some sense into Jennifer. Pleasure tingled through him. Involuntarily he licked his lips. Her taste no longer lingered there, but it was branded on his memory.

When he'd said good-night last evening, after a pleasant dinner at the Firehouse restaurant in Rapid City, hope had flooded his heart. Had Jennifer begun to regret the kiss? Had regret spun her mood into the fury of a tornado?

He intended to find out.

He checked between the rickety slats of the bunkhouse steps for unwanted visitors of the slinky type. Nothing. Brett tromped up the stairs. The weather-worn planks threatened to snap under his weight. Good thing he didn't plan on sneaking up on her.

She'd left the door ajar. Pushing it open, Brett allowed his eyes time to adjust to the shadowy light in the room. Stale air and musty dirt settled in his nose. He gingerly looked around the door. Plastic tarps covered all the furniture.

He took a few steps inside, eyes to the floor, ears keen to a warning rattle.

"You know they can crawl up a wall and drop from the rafters." Jennifer's factual statement echoed off the walls.

Brett's necked snapped back. He peered into the open rafters of the bunkhouse. A shiver ran through him. Something started to crawl around his arm. He closed his eyes, stifling a scream. He didn't want to be afraid in front of Jennifer, but fear groaned from his throat. There was a snake on him.

Leaden feet and weak knees made it impossible to turn around. Immediately he started to shake his arm. The snake's scaly flesh came in direct contact with Brett's forearm because he hadn't changed out of his polo shirt into long sleeves. He jerked his arm hard. The snake didn't come off. It kept wrapping itself around his bare forearm. The hair on his arm and at the base of his neck stood at attention from the creepy feel of the slithering reptile. He hadn't felt it fall on him, so he must have picked it up coming through the tall grass, his leather boots and heavy denims shielding the movement from its slimy ascent.

Then he heard it. A noise other than the high-pitched humming coming from his throat. He stopped all movement.

Jennifer's giggles rattled through the rafters and bounced off the walls of the bunkhouse. Humiliation's fiery heat surged through him. She'd done it again.

"That isn't funny." His words came out in a ragged huff. Sweat trickled down his back, and forehead. His heart still hammered in his chest. He turned in a half circle to face her.

She didn't stop laughing. She rolled the stem of a long piece of prairie grass, its silky bloomed seed head swirling in the air, its feathery ends mocking him. "Stalkers get what stalkers deserve," she said. She shrugged, flashing him a wry smile.

He felt another low growl forming in his throat, this time from attraction rather than fear. "I believe my being a stalker rescued you once."

The wry smile turned into disgusted pursed lips. "Why are you here?" she demanded.

"Why are you here?" Brett shot back in the same snotty tone. He removed his hat, the band sweat-soaked. He ran his fingers through his hair, lifting up and out to untangle his curls.

She pulled her mouth to the side, and smoothed some of the grass's sticky seed off of her yellow T-shirt and boot-cut jeans with her free hand. "I think we should use this to house the inner-city kids."

"It won't work. They need a chaperone."

Silently, Jennifer pointed her finger at Brett.

"Stop trying to get me out of the house." Brett shook his head. She wasn't getting rid of him. A deal was a deal. "But there are four boys and four girls. The girls require a female chaperone."

"Can't one of your graduate students do that?"

"No, they are working on dissertations. This is completely separate from their work."

Jennifer's shoulder's sagged. "I thought this might enhance their experience." She rubbed her dewy lips together.

She actually looked and sounded genuine.

"Is it safe?" Brett looked around the large open kitchen and living room area.

"Except for the front stairs. However I think your real question is 'Is it snake-free?'" Jennifer wrinkled her nose and smiled when she walked past him, the same taunting way she had in high school.

He raised an eyebrow, trying hard not to let her know that his heart still pounded in his chest from fear and hurt. She knew the weakness of his masculinity. No wonder she'd never considered him boyfriend material. He wanted her to see his strengths, not his weaknesses.

"No, I meant is it safe? No leaky gas line to the range.

The septic and well are in working order." Brett managed to keep the lingering fear out of his voice.

"I don't know. Eldon would have to answer those questions. By the ranch's books, I'm guessing the last time anyone stayed here was over three years ago. I can't find any payroll records for a hired hand since that time. I actually came out here to see if this could be turned into some kind of bed-and-breakfast for people who want the experience of a working ranch. Then I thought that the two large bunk rooms on opposite ends of the building would make great quarters for the kids."

It took all of Brett's bravado to walk normally across the length of the house to check out the bedroom areas, while his eyes darted to the nooks and crannies of the room. Between his fear of snakes and what most people considered a geeky occupation, Jennifer's blue eyes would never shine with love for him. Although, yesterday, after their kiss, something had flickered through them. But in an instant it had been gone.

Side by side, they stood staring into the bedroom. Built-in bunk beds, two beds in each frame, lined three walls. "I think you're right," he said, "but the girls have to have a woman chaperone. Cynthia's always filled that duty, but I don't think you're going to get her to come out here and sleep on those hard boards in a sleeping bag." Brett shivered at the thought himself. "And since you're not in her good graces right now, good luck trying to talk her into it."

Jennifer puckered her mouth, drawing it over to the side, before shrugging. "My life is in Chicago. I haven't dealt with ranch business in a long time. I am doing my best in a difficult situation. I'm sorry if I got short with everyone, but wearing so many hats is starting to weigh heavy on my head." She pointed to her temple. "If you know what I mean."

"I do know." He'd watched her grow wearier with each passing day. He'd had no idea she'd analyzed the ranch's books, in addition to all of her other responsibilities, until she'd mentioned the last time her dad hired ranch help.

"You need a hired hand. Running a ranch is a job and a half. Keeping up with your work at the magazine is another full-time job."

"So is the media frenzy in the pasture. What started out to be a blessing is becoming a nightmare with liability paperwork, extra insurance premiums and veterinary bills. Yet I feel an obligation to let everyone see what some consider a sacred sign." She shook her head. Sadness clouded her eyes when she found Brett's gaze. "I don't think the white buffalo is *my* sign, though."

How could Brett make her see that faith in Jesus, not in herself or a sign, is what made things happen. He knew she'd learned the words of Matthew 17:20: *Because you have so little faith. I tell you the truth, if you have faith as small as a mustard seed, you can say to this mountain, 'Move from here to there' and it will move. Nothing will be impossible for you.* His mother had taught them in vacation Bible school. But how had the message slipped by her?

"Why don't you come to church with me on Sunday? Mom would love it."

"I went to that church the first week I was home. I'll go again when I make it through my rotation."

Brett fought the urge to roll his eyes. He moved back to the center of the large combined kitchen, living and dining room. Faith had seven churches, and Jennifer attended a different one each Sunday. She'd started that routine when she learned to drive. He did the math. "If you went to our church the first week you were here, then by my calculations, you should be starting over."

Jennifer shook her head. "Last week Lance invited me to a worship service by the white buffalo pen."

Although Brett understood everyone's walk with God was unique to the individual, he felt certain that Jennifer was missing the faith element.

Jennifer scuffed her heels while circling him, walking around the room. "We could have it cleaned up in a few days. The kids could roll their sleeping bags out on the bunk beds. There are six in each room, so that's plenty. Let's do it." She faced him, hands on her hips in a determined stance.

"That idea is good in theory, but we need a female chaperone. We've always used the attic for the boys and the main floor of the house for the girls. It's worked out fine." Brett stuck his hands in the air in a stick-up fashion.

"We have a female chaperone."

"Who?

"Me." Her voice and expression were earnest.

Brett didn't mean to laugh. He tried to stop it, but a chuckle slipped from his throat. Even when she narrowed her eyes at him, he couldn't stop. He finally choked out, "Okay, let's try it."

Jennifer began to tick off everything they'd need to do to ready the bunkhouse for the kids, and Brett shook his head in wonder.

Eight kids, two adults, one bathroom and a makeup maven. He should go talk to one of the television stations covering the white buffalo calf because this was the stuff reality television was made of.

A few days later, Eldon pulled the chain to activate the water release on one of the outside showers. Water sprayed down from the wide flat showerhead. "See? We didn't need to buy camping showers." He walked down to the second stall and yanked the chain to release water. He repeated it on the third. "The boys should be set."

"Jennifer and I will split the girls up between the bathrooms in the ranch house for their bathing schedule." Cynthia clapped her hands together. "We should have thought of using these outside bunkhouse showers years ago instead of trying to rotate eight preteens through two bathrooms."

"You can say that again." Brett pushed his fedora to the back of his head, exposing his curl-covered forehead to the warm sunshine. Curls Jennifer longed to run her fingers through.

"Couldn't have." Eldon shrugged. "Had hired hands in here up until…" His voice trailed off. He lowered his eyes, suddenly interested in the dirt divot that the toe of his pointed boot dug when he wiggled it.

"Three years ago." Jennifer finished his sentence. "I've been going over the books. I know the last time that dad hired someone." Jennifer held her hands in the air. "I'd have known sooner if I'd stayed longer than a couple of days during the holidays when I came home." She'd discovered that the best way to counter everyone's criticism was to beat them to it.

"Well." Eldon shrugged, lifting his brown eyes to hers, his gravelly voice gruff.

"Every time I called Dad, he gave me the impression things were the same as when I'd left for college. My holiday visits were always short, so we spent the time catching up." Jennifer looked from Eldon to Cynthia. "Now I know why he never came to Chicago to visit me. He used the agricultural calendar—time to cut hay, time to move the herd—as an excuse when really it boiled down to his finances."

"I came to see you in Chicago." Lance walked up behind the group watching the water spray down from the shower, damping the cement pad underneath but not dousing the flames of unspoken blame.

"Shouldn't you be out playing in the dirt?" Lance gave Brett's shoulder a little more than a playful punch. "Instead of hanging around my girl."

Brett's body tensed. He stretched to his full height. Jennifer thought she saw smoke come out of Brett's ears. "Your mother's great company," Brett said in an even and matter of fact tone.

"Good one." Lance chuckled. "But we all know I meant Jennifer."

"What is it you want, son?" Cynthia walked over to Lance, wrapping him in a big hug, putting her body between the two men.

"If you'll excuse me, I'll go back inside and get started cleaning the kitchen range." Brett stepped around Cynthia. "Are you going to help me?" he asked Jennifer as he walked past her.

"Naw, she wants to come with me. The tribal members from California are leaving. We're going into Faith for a bite to eat, see what's happening in town." Lance broke free of Cynthia's embrace. "I think Jennifer's been working too hard. She needs some relaxation. What do you say? It'll be like old times."

Lance might have been talking to Jennifer, but he was looking past her at Brett. After twelve years, you'd think he'd have grown up and stopped his goading, especially after what Brett had done for him. Them.

The soft swish of denim stopped. Jennifer guessed Brett had turned around, weight on his left leg, his right leg slightly bent. Fedora pushed back and his hand on his hips, so the stare-down could begin. She'd seen this macho display many times before. Brett lost every time. Yet,

Lance's offer wasn't even tempting. Growing up, she'd jumped at any chance to go to town; now she found the solitude of the ranch much nicer.

Her body stiffened. *She found the solitude of the ranch nicer than the bustle of the city?*

"I believe she has dinner plans." Brett's voice carried across the quiet plains, snapping Jennifer back into the conversation.

"I do?" She turned around, finding Brett's stance exactly how she'd imagined it.

"Yes, you do," Brett answered, never breaking eye contact with Lance.

"Mom won't care if she misses dinner. Will you, Mom?" Lance called over his shoulder.

"That is not my decision. It's Jennifer's."

"Why don't you go on into town, son? We've got a lot of work to do." Eldon moved closer to Lance.

Jennifer's eyes widened. Surely they didn't think these two were going to have a fistfight over her dinner plans. Plans she didn't even know she had.

"Come on, Jennifer, let's go." Lance reached out his hand, taking a step toward her.

Faster than a whip's snap, Brett stood beside her, his firm bicep brushing against her back. His arm wrapped around her shoulder.

When Brett turned, intending for both of them to leave, her left foot caught on her right boot causing her to stumble. She hadn't meant to keep her feet so firmly planted on the ground.

Lance laughed out loud.

Tension bulged Brett's bicep. He slipped his hand from her shoulder and before she knew it both of his hands secured her waist, lifting her until her feet dangled inches from the rocky dirt around the bunkhouse. Face-to-face, she saw the determined set to Brett's chin. The fierce emotion in his brown eyes, which she'd witnessed once before, had nothing to do with anger or Lance.

"Indy, let her go so she can come and have some fun with me and my friends." Lance took another step toward them.

The corners of Brett's lips turned up into his cocky smile. He glanced over at Lance. "Not this time."

The commanding tone of his voice sent a shiver of delight through her, and she giggled.

Her merriment drew Brett's attention back to her. He dipped his head, his lips landing on hers. Her eyes rounded in surprise at his display of affection. When his eyelids fluttered shut, Jennifer followed his lead. Their kiss deepened.

The warm summer breeze swirled the sweet scent of cut alfalfa through the air. Before she was ready, Brett ended the kiss, gently returning her to the solid ground. Her legs shook. She felt like a newborn calf trying to stand.

Brett's hand grazed the length of her arm. His fingers glided along her palm until they interlocked with hers. He turned to Lance. "She's mine now. Leave her alone."

He guided her into a turn and walked away with the short determined steps of a fearless man. Jennifer's heart flipped. They rounded the end of the bunkhouse stepping up to the door in silence.

At the threshold, she pulled her hand free. "What...?" She lost her train of thought when Brett turned to face her, sheepishness etched in his features.

"I'm sorry. I meant to end this evening with a kiss, not start it with one."

Jennifer pulled her brows tight, frowning. "What?" Her attraction to Brett fogged her mind.

"Actually, that isn't really the kiss I planned to end the evening with, either. This is." Brett ran his palms over her cheeks. Cradling her face in a gentle embrace, he bent down. A soft tender kiss landed on her lips, and tickled her heart until it skipped through her chest. Her pulse resounding in her ears rivaled the ceremonial drums over the knoll.

When the kiss ended, Jennifer lifted her eyes and searched Brett's face. Her heart boomed harder at the sparkle in his eyes.

"But, since I can't get anything right when I'm around you, this is not the right door to kiss you good-night in front of, either." The corner of his mouth curved into a lopsided grin. "Would you join me for dinner?"

He opened the screen door and pushed the heavy wooden door of the bunkhouse open. Jennifer peeked around the door frame. The wooden planks of the floor were scrubbed clean. A lace tablecloth covered a small round table with two chairs. A vase filled with wildflowers sat in the center surrounded by a table setting for two.

She sighed softly, and stepped inside. "Do I smell your mother's fried chicken?"

"That depends on if that sigh means yes, you'll have dinner with me."

Jennifer had reached the table. She fingered the lace tablecloth. "Did you do all of this for me?"

"I had some help. I know it's not a four-star restaurant like you're used to but…"

Her abrupt turn silenced him. "It's wonderful. I would love to share supper with you."

"Go wash up." The corner of Brett's mouth curled into the cocky grin that Jennifer had wanted to slap off his face for many years. Now the sight of it warmed her heart.

Jennifer entered the bathroom. Catching her reflection in the mirror, she groaned. She'd forgotten that she'd slipped on one of her dad's old front-pocketed T-shirts. The faded green cotton sleeves' seams hung off of her shoulders a good two inches. The shine on her nose needed powdering. Her lips needed a dash of color with a coat of gloss, and her makeup was a football field away in the main house.

"What's the matter?" Brett filled the open doorway. Their eyes met in the mirror; a trace of judgment ran through his eyes before they softened. "You look beautiful. Now come to supper."

Supper. A term she'd long ago dropped after receiving ghastly looks from her coworkers in the city. Dinner in the city consisted of trendy food and stilted conversation. Supper brought visions of comfort food and family camaraderie to her mind.

Brett waited behind her chair, easing it forward until she was tucked securely in place. A platter of fried chicken, buttermilk biscuits, homemade potato chips and cabbage slaw filled the small table. "All of my favorites."

The wooden floor creaked when Brett scooted his chair close to the table. He looked at the platter of chicken and said in a funny voice that would crack the kids up, "Hey, birdie, I think she was talking to me."

Without thinking twice, Jennifer answered, "I was."

For a moment Brett's face showed his surprise at her response; then his lips curled into his cocky grin.

Chapter 9

Jennifer stood back, surveying the finished bunkhouse. "Not bad." She nodded her head, looking around the shared common area.

"I had my doubts." Cynthia lifted folded towels from a laundry basket.

"Well, at least one thing has worked out for me." She straightened a picture they'd found in storage in the basement of the main house.

"I'd say two things." Cynthia walked back into the great room, wiggling her eyebrows.

A blush bloomed on Jennifer's cheeks. She waved off Cynthia's comment with her hand. "That was to get back at Lance."

"So you keep telling me, with blushes glowing on your cheeks." Cynthia sat on the couch. "But Lance hasn't been around for a week, and you're still spending any free time you have together."

Jennifer had turned her back to Cynthia, peering out of the sparkling-clean window toward the lane that branched off from the main house. Brett had been gone forever.

"Have a seat. It'll be a while before he gets back."

A little thrill twirled inside Jennifer when she tried to purse her lips, but a grin won out. "I'm anxious for the kids to get here so I can see their reactions to the bunkhouse." Jennifer turned from her lookout post.

"I don't doubt that, but they are not who you are waiting for." Cynthia arched a brow.

Jennifer smiled at her surrogate mother's teasing, and sat down on the sofa beside her. "It is nice to finally have something in common with Brett. We both enjoy working with kids."

"You have more in common with Brett than that. You grew up in the same area, went to the same school, have shared experiences."

"I have all of that in common with a lot of people, including Lance, but that doesn't mean anything anymore."

"Lance is not a good example. He has amends to make before his past is a pleasant memory." Cynthia's pointed look at Jennifer was a reminder that she had her own amends to make.

Jennifer shook her head. "I never had much in common with anyone here. I was always a misfit. At least in the city I fit in." Even as the words tumbled out, Jennifer knew they weren't entirely true. Sure, no one looked at her with pity in their eyes because she had no mother. Yet many aspects of city life had been hard for her to adjust to, some more apparent than others. She'd been unaware of the anonymity issue until that morning in Rapid City.

"It is true that people grow apart but still have things in common," Cynthia said. "Links to the past that will bind you together forever, like the arrowheads, teeth and pottery on Brett's dig site. Whoever lived here and left those behind helped form this land that we now call home."

The crackle of tires over gravel stopped their conversation.

"They're here." Jennifer jumped up from the couch, ran to the door and threw it open wide.

Brett had traded his SUV for a twelve-person van, with the School of Mines insignia. When he opened the door and slid from the driver's seat, Jennifer heard a loud rendition of a traveling song.

He rounded the van, stopping to open the double back doors, still singing along with the kids. The children opened the side door and began leaping out of the van.

The culturally diverse group of boys and girls stood wide-eyed, taking in their surroundings. "There is so much sky here." A boy's voice, on the verge of changing, cracked.

"Grab your bags out of the back and head to the house," Brett instructed. "I'm sure there are refreshments ready for you, although—" he reached into the van and removed a large plastic bag filled with empty fruit snacks and juice boxes "—I'm sure none of you are hungry."

"I could eat," one boy piped up. A chorus of voices agreed.

Jennifer held the door open. The children tromped up the stairs, entering the bunkhouse. A young girl, the last in line, stopped, pushing her glasses up her nose. She smiled at Jennifer. "There's buffalo down by the road." Her voice held such awe that Jennifer couldn't help but laugh.

Brett walked up behind her and patted the girl's shoulder. "Rajean, this lady owns those buffalo."

The girl's eyes grew even bigger through her magnified lenses. "Really?"

"Actually—" Jennifer motioned for the girl to enter the

house "—my father owns them. He runs cattle, too. I'm here helping for the summer."

"Do you got horses, too?" a boy asked while munching on his cookie, sending crumbs flying through the air.

"No, they don't *have* horses." Brett tousled the young man's blond hair. "Alex, mind your manners and don't talk with your mouth full, okay?"

Alex made a show of swallowing, while shaking his head. "Okay."

Jennifer's heart warmed at Brett's crooked smile and easy rapport with the children. He was a natural teacher. She suspected that Alex hadn't even realized that his grammar had been corrected or his actions slightly reprimanded.

"Okay, everyone got a cookie and milk?"

The kids nodded their heads. "Time for introductions. This is Cynthia. She'll be cooking all of your meals."

"Are you an Indian?" Rajean asked.

"Full Lakota." Cynthia smiled at the girl. "So is my husband, Eldon, but we prefer being called Native American or indigenous people."

"Indigenous? What does that mean?" Alex asked.

"It means that their people were in America before other people immigrated to America."

Most of the children frowned at Brett's definition.

"He means the pilgrims," Alex said.

Brett smiled at Alex's clarification and continued with the introductions.

"This is Jennifer. Her family owns this ranch. She'll be staying in the bunks with the girls." Brett snagged a cookie and a cup of milk.

"Wow, you grew up here? You're lucky."

The wonder in the boy's tone struck a chord in Jennifer's heart. At his age, she'd felt lucky to rove the land, discovering the mysteries it held. Pheasant nests in the spring, a herd of wild antelope hidden in a thicket of trees, bobcat tracks in fresh mud. As she'd grown older, though, her feelings had altered. The ranch had changed from a place of wonder to a prison when she realized that all their neighbors pitied the little girl without a mother.

"Okay." Brett held up a hand. "They know that you all live in Kansas City, Missouri, but what they don't know is your names. When I touch your head, introduce yourself."

"Rajean." The girl pushed her glasses up her nose then ran her fingers over the tight rows of braids in her wiry hair.

"Alex."

Jennifer wondered if the fair-haired, fair-skinned boy had brought along sunscreen. She made a mental note to make sure all the children wore it while out at the dig site.

"Carlie." The girl towered over everyone, even with her slouched shoulders and slouched posture.

"Jose and Carmen." Their fraternal resemblance was apparent, with eyes the color of the chocolate chips in the cookies they devoured.

"Tiffany."

The petite girl appeared uncomfortable, and pulled at the oversize shirt she wore. Jennifer suspected early puberty caused her discomfort.

"Brandon."

"Riley."

The last two boys' cropped hair and long noses gave away that they were brothers. Not twins, like Jose and Carmen, but Jennifer guessed only about ten months separated their ages.

"What a fine-looking crew!" Cynthia clapped her hands together. "It's very nice to meet you all."

"Yes, it is." Jennifer followed Cynthia's response.

"Do we get to start digging today?" Alex put his empty cup on the table.

"No, but I'll show you the dig site."

"Do you think we'll discover another Sue T-Rex or some type of dinosaur bones?" Alex danced from one foot to the other.

"What's that?" Rajean asked.

"Didn't you read about the area before you came here?" The disbelief in Alex's voice brought a grin to Brett's face. His gaze found Jennifer's; she knew the look. Brett was going to talk about his favorite subject.

"Come over here." Brett sat on the floor in front of the sofa. The kids gathered around him. "Not far from here, in bluffs similar to the ones you saw outside, an archeologist found an entire skeleton of a tyrannosaurus rex. It's on display at the Field Museum in Chicago."

"Isn't that awesome?" Alex pumped his fist. "Did you help dig it out?"

"No, I was about your age, but I did get to watch the excavation."

Jennifer recalled the media frenzy and onlookers, similar to the ones camped at the property line of the ranch now.

"Will we get to dig a dinosaur out of the rocks, too?" Jose's face was so earnest, Jennifer was filled with a new appreciation of what had put their town of Faith on the map.

"I don't know. We never know what treasures lay beneath the surface of rocks and dirt. There is another dig site on this ranch where they've found arrowheads, broken pottery and teeth, which led them to uncover a line of rocks they think was the foundation of a building at one time."

"Maybe we'll find gold!" Alex proclaimed. "The Black Hills are known for that."

"Really?" Carmen clapped her hands.

"Sorry, gang, there's no gold here. I'm guessing we'll find fossils, though." Brett winked at Jennifer. She knew he'd been out scouting the area around the bluffs for signs of fossils so the kids wouldn't get disappointed during their two-week stay.

"Let's get our gear put away. Then we'll walk down and get a closer look at that white buffalo calf. Girls, you follow Jennifer. Guys, this way." Brett hitched his thumb toward the boys' bunk.

"You look familiar," Carlie said as she lifted her bag to her shoulders and stepped closer to Jennifer.

"I thought so, too," Tiffany added, looking at Jennifer. She carried her bag with both hands in front of her. The bump of her knees caused it to swing forward with each step. "But I've never been here before so how can I know you, right?"

"She's only here for the summer." Rajean stepped up beside the other girls. "Isn't that right?"

"Yes, that's right. I live and work in Chicago." Jennifer tried to usher the girls toward their area in the bunkhouse.

"What do you do there?" Carmen asked.

"I'm a journalist…" Jennifer stopped in midsentence. She couldn't be sure, but through the shuffling of bags, she thought she heard a soft snort. Her head jerked in Brett's direction. He dropped his eyes before hers made contact. After all the pleasant time they'd spent together, he still didn't respect her work. "At a magazine…"

Tiffany's bag thudded down on the wooden floorboards. She squatted, whizzing the zipper open. "I knew it." She pulled a copy of *Transitions* from her bag, flipping through the pages until she found the beauty column. "It's you!" She folded it open and pointed to Jennifer's picture and byline at the bottom of the page.

"It's me." Jennifer smiled. All the kids gathered around the magazine.

"I read your column every month, but now I'm going to read it first. Will you autograph my magazine?"

"Sure."

"I love the advice you give on makeup." Carlie stood a little straighter. "My mom let me buy some mascara this summer." She fluttered her eyelashes.

Jennifer inspected her face. "You did a good job of applying it."

The echo of Brett clearing his throat bounced through the rafters. Jennifer looked up from the excited group around her into the disapproving stare she'd been seeing for years. Her heart sagged. She was gaining respect for his work, but it was apparent that he'd never respect her work.

Brett left the boys to fight over who got the top bunks, and went outside. After a quick check of the area under and around the steps, he sat on the first step. It'd never crossed his mind that the preteen girls would be readers of *Transitions*. His knee-jerk reaction to Jennifer's reference to being a journalist had erased the relationship that'd been developing over the past two weeks if Jennifer's glare was any indication.

The quick slap of the cushioned soles of Jennifer's boots on the floor resonated with anger. She pushed through the door; the edge of the screen knocked into him.

"Hey." Brett stood, rubbing his shoulder.

Jennifer squeezed through the narrow opening. "Sorry." She pushed past him, thundering down the stairs.

"You don't sound very sorry."

"Well—" Jennifer spun around "—I am sorry. I'm sorry my dad had a stroke, and I had to come back to a place where no one respects my career choice."

Brett jumped from the top stair, grabbed Jennifer by the arm and dragged her away from the house. "Keep your voice down." His voice more of a growl than he'd intended.

"Let go of me." Jennifer spoke through clenched teeth, before she jerked her arm free of his grasp.

"I'm sorry that I made that noise when the girls recognized you."

Astonishment crept over Jennifer's features. "Really?"

"Yes, really."

Jennifer tugged at the sleeve of her red gingham Western shirt. "They want me to give them makeovers."

"What?" Brett's bellow filled the silence. He clenched his fists, then lowered his voice. "What did you say?"

"Maybe, if we have time."

"They're here to learn about archeology, not fluff." Brett leaned against the back of the van; pulling one leg up, he rested his foot on the bumper.

Jennifer planted herself directly in front of him. "Fluff? Cosmetics companies earn billions of dollars a year enhancing women's beauty."

"That's where our opinions differ. Most women cover up their beauty rather than enhance it. Look at my mom." Brett wished he'd put his fedora on—the hot sun beat down in his eyes.

"Your mom?"

"Yeah, my mom. Her bright red cheeks and lips, blue or green eye shadow, colored-in eyebrows. Do you have any idea of what she looks like without makeup?"

Jennifer shook her head. "I don't."

"Her skin is ivory with naturally pink cheeks. Her brows and lashes are light brown."

"You resemble her?"

Brett laughed out loud at her astonishment. "You'd never know it, would you? Growing up, people would look at our family, and I'm sure they thought I was adopted. Dad with his olive skin and jet-black hair from his French Canadian heritage, Mom all made up with bronzer on her face, trying to match his skin tones."

Jennifer dropped her eyes, then slowly lifted them to meet his eyes. "I wondered."

"But under all of that of that fluff, my mom's a wonderful person. I don't know why she hides behind layers of makeup."

Raising her hand to her chest, Jennifer's mouth dropped. "Is that what you think about me?"

Chapter 10

Before Brett could answer Jennifer's question, the children burst from the bunkhouse ready to go see the white bison calf. So Jennifer spent the rest of the day squirrelled away inside her dad's office trying to concentrate on her column, which was nearly impossible with their earlier conversation replaying in her mind.

He thought she hid behind her makeup? Imagine that! Yet a niggling of doubt invaded her thoughts.

Her college professor had encouraged her to try her hand at creative nonfiction. She'd had some success placing articles in regional publications until she landed the intern position at *Transitions* that eventually led to the beauty columnist job. Angry and determined to prove Brett wrong, she typed a pitch for a nonfiction article and shot off an email to Jacque. Then doubt set in while she worked on her column. Did she even remember how to write about something besides beauty? A Christmas story idea spun through her mind. She opened a new document and began typing.

A knock sounded on the door. "Jennifer. It's almost time for the girls to head to the bunkhouse for the night."

Frowning, Jennifer lifted her eyes from the laptop screen. The fading light of the day caught the slats of the mini blinds, casting shadows in the corner of the room. She glanced at the corner of the computer screen. Lost in her work, she hadn't realized how much time had passed.

She gathered up her notes and laptop, dropping them into her bag. Cynthia stood right outside the door holding a meatloaf sandwich on a paper plate. "You missed dinner." She pushed the plate toward Jennifer. "The main floor shower is free, but you need to hurry. The girls are supposed to be settled into bed by nine."

Cynthia held her left arm out for Jennifer to see her watch.

"And you'll probably be taking a tepid shower, at best."

Nodding, Jennifer grabbed the plate, and hurried down the hall to her room. The murmur of the girls voices, and high-pitched giggles filled the living room.

After a quick shower, Jennifer slipped into her light-weight pajamas decorated with various breeds of cartoon-ish dogs. She rummaged through her closet for a gag gift Lance had given her for Christmas years ago. If her memory served, the box was on the top shelf tucked into the back corner. Jennifer removed the cover, pulling out slippers fashioned in the shape of a dog. She slipped them on. The head of the dog was on her toes, the tail tickling the back of her ankle. Granted they were winter slippers but the hard sole was perfect for walking back to the bunkhouse on the crushed red rock driveway.

With the flapping tongued beagles on her feet, she walked into the living room, striking a pose. A riot of giggles filled the room. The howls and barking laughter continued all the way down to the bunkhouse.

She held the door while the girls, adorned in various styles and shades of robes, marched through single file into the combination kitchen and living room. The boys, gathered around the table engrossed in a board game, didn't look up at the pajama parade.

Brett's glance turned into a double take. "Jennifer, I guess you must have been on your feet most of the day. Your dogs are a barkin'."

He laughed, slapping his leg. No one joined him. Eight sets of eyes stared at him, questioning his sanity. His groaner had backfired.

"It's an old expression that means your feet hurt. Since I have—" Jennifer lifted one foot high "—dog slippers."

"That was a *bad* one. No high five for you." Alex's attention turned back to the board game. Brett's laughter wound down, ending in a sigh.

The rest of the boys turned back to their game. The girls circled the table to watch the game when a high-pitched beeping came from Brett's pocket.

He pulled out his phone. "Bedtime alarm. Everyone knows where the bathroom is, right?"

The group nodded, some through sleep-laden eyes.

"It's off to bed then. I suggest that you keep the midnight whispers to a minimum. Wake-up call is seven o'clock sharp."

Jennifer herded the girls toward their bedroom. After everyone was on their bunks snuggled into sleeping bags, she adjusted the temperature of the window air conditioner.

"Good night."

"I thought you were staying here with us." Rajean rose up on her elbow.

"I am. I have some work to do, but come seven o'clock you'll find me right there." Jennifer pointed to a lower bunk covered with a downy sleeping bag.

Rajean frowned. "What's that noise?"

The buzzing vibrations of a cicada filled the night air. "It's an insect."

Rajean's lip quivered. Jennifer added hastily, "That's outside probably high in the tree we walked by on our way to the bunkhouse. There's nothing to be afraid of. I'm right outside if you need me."

Jennifer said a prayer that a pack of coyotes wouldn't start yelping during the night and frighten Rajean. She pulled on the door, leaving the tiniest sliver of an opening.

Brett sat with his back against the arm of the couch. His legs stretched across the length of the cushions. An open laptop rested on a blue lap desk. His bare feet stuck out of his black jersey athletic pants.

"Are they settled in?"

"Yes." Jennifer padded across the floor, slipped her laptop from the bag and stepped over to the overstuffed chair. Using the tips of her toes, she removed her cartoon slippers. She folded her legs under her, wishing she had a portable desk to help deflect the heat that radiated from her laptop.

"Working on your column?" Brett asked without looking up from his screen. His fingers still tapping keys.

"No, actually, I'm not. A recent conversation sparked a story idea."

Brett's fingers stilled. He peered over the screen, brows raised.

"What are you working on?" Jennifer pretended not to notice his facial response.

"An article for a trade magazine on bringing the inner-city kids here for a dig." Brett yawned and stretched.

"Hmm…" Everyone in the writing field knew there were no original ideas. Unique delivery breathed fresh life into a subject. "Will your article include pictures?" Jennifer lowered her laptop screen.

"Some. The release for picture use is covered in the application the kids file to be considered as a dig candidate." Brett lowered his eyes to his screen. His fingers tapped the keyboard, the clickity click filling the silence in the room.

"What's the slant of your article?"

"The socio-economic aspect of giving children a polar opposite environment in which to learn." Again Brett yawned and stretched. "I do believe that the day is catching up to me."

He closed his laptop, balancing it on the arm of the sofa. "Before I turn in I think we should finish the conversation we started this afternoon."

He swung his legs off the couch, scooting to the end closest to Jennifer.

She rubbed her lips together, the surface slick with lip balm. Sometime during the afternoon she'd come to terms with Brett's opinion of her shallowness. It didn't mean she liked it, but she could accept it.

Leaning forward, Brett rested his forearms on his knees, his hands dangling in the air.

"I didn't mean to imply that you are superficial. I don't think that at all, but…" He paused and lifted his hands in a questioning gesture. "I'm not so sure it's not the signal you send the world."

Jennifer opened her mouth. Brett held up a halting hand.

"You are smart, talented and beautiful. When you get it in your head to do something, you make it happen. I mean, look at this place. No one would know that just two weeks ago it'd been uninhabited for years."

The room did sparkle from several scrubbings. The range and refrigerator looked new, even though they'd get little use during the course of the kids' two-week stay. Pictures hung on the walls, relieving the starkness of the dark paneling that had been popular in the seventies. Throw pillows and bean bag chairs dotted the floor like polka dots on a clown's tie, giving the room a cozy, kid-friendly atmosphere.

"Thank you." Jennifer gave her a head a curt nod. Irritation buzzed through her, zeroing in on his earlier implication of her shallowness rather than on his compliments. "And thank you for the air mattresses on the bunks."

"Jennifer, don't try to sidetrack this conversation. There's more to you than you let people see. You're brave, strong and independent. The only time you show that side of your personality is when you are riled up."

"Which is starting to happen," Jennifer snapped. She guided her feet into her slippers before walking across the room. She slipped her laptop into her bag. She was no longer in the mood to work. She turned, blinking her eyes rapidly to remove the threat of tears. Maybe she *hadn't* come to terms with or accepted Brett's opinion. It had never mattered to her before what he thought—why did it now?"

She purposely kept her voice even and low, so she didn't disturb the children. "Brett, you've had a charmed life. In so many words you said so the other day. You don't know how it feels to see pity in everyone's eyes when they look at you because you're a little girl with no mother. In my heart I pitied myself, too. Then your mom befriended me, and I wanted to emulate her because when she looked at me, all I saw was love and acceptance."

Brett hung his head, his hair tumbling forward, creating a waterfall of waves over his forehead. Curls her fingers itched to smooth away from his handsome face even in her agitated state. She clamped her hands together behind her back. That's why his opinion bothered her. She'd developed feelings for him, and wanted them reciprocated.

"A trait that you didn't inherit from her, I might add." Her voice was as snotty as she could muster through a whisper.

Time seemed to move in slow motion, yet it only took a second for Brett's head to snap up, curls bouncing around his ears.

"Every time you look at me I know that you're judging my choices."

"That's not true." He stood, taking a step toward her. "Since I was thirteen years old, I wanted you to notice me because, believe me, I noticed you."

When he reached her, he grazed his hands over her arms, loosening her grip until her hands dangled at her side. He entwined his fingers with hers. "I don't know how judgment can shine from my eyes when love warms my heart every time I look at you. Don't think all of your rebuffs and teasing didn't hurt me over the years. I kept following you around, hoping you'd change your mind and like me."

A sly twinkle winked from his brown eyes; his lips curved into that familiar grin. This time, the slight curl of his lips didn't raise her ire. The dim glow of the bunkhouse cast a different light on his smile, making Jennifer realize it wasn't cocky but apprehensive.

"Did you just say that you loved me?" she whispered in disbelief.

"I did." Brett kissed her forehead, then rested his

against hers, looking her directly in the eyes. "I always have, and that's why I went to jail for you."

When Brett walked into the great room at precisely six fifty-five the next morning, he found Jennifer zonked out on the couch in a sitting position, with Rajean stretched across the cushion, feet resting in Jennifer's lap.

It must have been a rough night for both of them. Disappointment in Jennifer's reaction to his declaration of love had kept him tossing and turning all night. Eyes wide with fear, she'd pulled free of his embrace. How could she not have seen the love in his eyes all these years? Why had he set himself up for rejection again?

He rubbed the sleep from his eyes with the knuckles of his index fingers. He knew a long day lay ahead.

He stepped over to shake Jennifer's shoulder, and she lifted her head and popped open one eye at the creak of the aged wood floor.

"It's seven already, isn't it?" The weariness in her voice confirmed his suspicion.

"Bad dream?" He squatted beside the green plaid sofa.

"Nope, scary noises." Jennifer stretched her arms before sliding Rajean's feet from her thighs.

"The coyotes?"

Jennifer nodded her head. "Kansas City can't be much different from Chicago with sirens blaring through the night or horns honking at all hours, but the yelp of the coyotes woke her up." A big sigh followed Jennifer's whisper.

"Those are familiar noises in a familiar place." Brett shrugged. "This might be her first time away from home."

"Yeah." Jennifer rubbed her chin. "I never thought of that." A slight smile crossed her lips. "I'll have to ask her, all of them."

Puzzled by her response, Brett started to ask her what she meant but never had the chance.

A blaringly loud buzzer sounded through the bunkhouse. Jennifer covered her ears. "You're going to scare them all to death," she shouted over the deafening noise.

Brett laughed. "You obviously don't remember how hard it is for kids to roll out of bed in the morning." He pointed to Rajean, who hadn't flinched.

Jennifer threw her hands in the air. "Coyotes at least three miles away wake her up, but this she can sleep through. Go turn it off. I'll get them out of bed."

"Nope, I don't turn it off until all of the kids are in a standing position. It only takes one to keep lying in bed to get us off schedule."

"What is that?" one of the boys groaned, his voice carrying through the open doorway.

"I think it's the fire alarm. Get everyone up," Alex cried.

Brett cocked an eyebrow and shrugged. "I'll take care of them. You get this one and the other girls."

"What is that noise?" Carlie came through the bedroom door, hands over her ears.

"Your wake-up call. Good morning, Carlie." Brett flashed her a bright smile but did not receive one in return.

"Carlie, are the other girls up?" Jennifer shook Rajean's shoulder. "He won't turn it off until there are ten pairs of feet on the floor."

The clump of boys ran into Brett's body trying to make their escape. "Great, you're up."

"Is there a fire?"

"Nope, the wake-up call." Brett shepherded the boys, clad in T-shirts and athletic shorts, to the common area.

Rajean started to stir.

"I'll go check on the other girls." Jennifer hurried into

the girls' bunk. Single file they followed her out into the living room, robes tied tight and hands over their ears.

"This is annoying," Carmen shouted.

Jennifer carried Rajean's robe to the couch. Rajean blinked her eyes a few times.

"What's going on?" She sat up, stretching her arms.

"Please put your feet on the floor." Jennifer helped her push one arm, then the other, into her robe.

Brett pulled a fob from his pocket, pressed a button and the noise stopped.

"Good morning." He laughed when his cheerful greeting was met with moans and groans. "What kind of insect likes to sleep late?"

Eight sleepy faces stared at him.

"A lazy bug." He chuckled at the kids' eye-rolls. "This is how we wake up every morning, so the sooner you're out of bed, the sooner the alarm stops. You have ten minutes to get dressed and be back out so we can head to the main house for breakfast."

Shrieking, the girls scurried off to their room, complaining that wasn't enough time. The boys sauntered toward their room grumbling about the noisy girls.

"That includes you." Brett gave Jennifer a pointed look, wondering how she'd pull her makeup routine off in such a short amount of time.

Jennifer zipped her laptop case. "My clothes are at the main house. I'm only sleeping here. I'll eat with the group, then get dressed and start my day after your troupe of future archeologists heads to the dig site. It's you who'd better hurry."

Surprise widened Brett's eyes. He'd never considered that option. He rushed to the boys' bunk, managing to dress in five minutes. He shooed the kids out the door ahead of him and Jennifer.

"Let me take that." He slung her laptop bag over his shoulder, then reached for her hand.

She laced her soft fingers through his, gently tugging on his arm to stop him. The kids continued to scramble toward the ranch house.

"About last night." Jennifer turned to face him. He pushed his fedora back on his head, bracing for what appeared to be bad news judging by the serious look on Jennifer's face.

He looked down, studying the eyelets on his worn leather lace-up boots. Fear of rejection had kept him tossing and turning all night. What was it about her that made him show his vulnerable side? He knew she had no intention of staying here, and this is where he chose to live his life.

"Would you look at me?"

With a deep sigh, he lifted his eyes to hers. She searched his face while he mentally prepared for the rejection that would surely come.

"I wanted to say thank you."

You've lived without her love for this long…

Jennifer's words began to sink in. Brett gave his head a slight shake. "I'm sorry, what did you say?"

Jennifer pursed her lips. "You are just trying to get me to say it again."

"Not really." Brett laughed. "I thought you were going to say something else."

"What?"

"Never mind. Let's start again." Brett leaned closer, enjoying the natural rosy glow that kissed Jennifer's cheeks, wishing his lips could do the same.

"I've never properly thanked you for what you did for me in high school. I'd have lost my scholarship if I'd have been caught with that can of spray paint."

"I know. That's why I did it. You wanted to get out of here so badly…" Brett's voice trailed off. *And she still does.*

"Thank you. I didn't realize it then, but it was a selfless act on your part."

"Not quite selfless." Brett wiggled his eyebrows.

Jennifer laughed. "I owed you more than a kiss that had so many stipulations attached to it. I'm sorry. I should have kissed you in the middle of Main Street for all of the world to see."

"You can still do that if you want to. I'm game."

Jennifer's eyes shot heavenward. She shook her head. "What I've never understood is why you didn't come clean about whom the spray paint actually belonged to."

"He had a scholarship, too, at a campus the opposite direction of the college *you* were attending. If he lost his and stayed around here…" Brett shrugged. "Well, let's just say I never understood what you saw in him as a friend. That wasn't the first time he left you to take the heat for his actions."

Years ago when Brett had pointed that out, hoping to gain her friendship, she'd argued with him. Today, she looked off in the direction of the white buffalo pen.

"I agree." She turned her attention back to Brett. "He owes us an apology. I didn't realize the principal would actually call the sheriff and have you hauled off to jail."

"I think he only did that because he knew it wasn't mine. He knew it belonged to Lance, but I wouldn't confirm it and, well, I was interested in archeology and hieroglyphics so he couldn't really argue that I might not have spray painted the Native American symbols on the school. They didn't keep me overnight. They released me into my parents' custody."

"Well, I know that you were grounded, and I'm sorry

about that. It's been bothering me since I arrived. I should have thanked you a lot sooner."

Brett leaned in and pecked a kiss on her pretty pink cheek. "You are welcome." She didn't declare her love for him, but the conversation wasn't the rejection he thought it'd be. It was taking time but they were clearing the air between them. That was a step in the right direction. "We'd better go get some breakfast before there isn't any left."

Jennifer planned to head to the dig site by midafternoon for some hands-on research for her nonfiction article, and to see Brett. However Eldon found a fence that needed mending, which left her to cut the alfalfa field during the time she'd planned to work on her column. She stopped the tractor by the machine shed, and jumped off.

Brett loved her. The thought brought a wide smile to her lips, and happiness coursed through her, making her almost skip across the yard to the house. Removing her straw cowboy hat, she wiped across her forehead with the long sleeve of her chambray shirt. The heat was brutal today. She hoped the kids were digging in shade. She knew Brett had coolers of water available.

A tall glass of water would hit the spot. Jennifer headed toward the house.

"Hello? Cynthia?" Jennifer called opening the back door, and stepping into the mud porch. When no answer came, Jennifer shrugged her shoulders. "Must be running errands in town." Jennifer looked down at her shirt speckled with sweat, topsoil and bits of alfalfa. In an effort to save money, she'd used the old tractor instead of the new one with the air-conditioned cab. "Lucky her," she muttered.

Jennifer tucked her gloves into her cowboy hat and hung it on a peg in the mudroom. She brushed her hands down the front of her shirt, slipped out of her boots and headed to the kitchen. She loaded a glass with ice before holding it under the tap. The cool liquid soothed her parched throat. While refilling her glass, her cell phone rang.

She pulled it from the front pocket of her shirt. Jacque's face and number flashed on the smartphone's screen. She hadn't missed a conference call, had she?

"Hello."

"Jennifer, don't you return calls anymore?" Jacque's frazzled voice echoed in Jennifer's ear. "I've left messages on your cell and landline."

"I didn't know that you'd called." Unable to see her cell indicators while connected to Jacque, Jennifer walked around the island in the kitchen until she could see the answering machine on an end table in the living room. A red light blinked that a message, or maybe two, were waiting. "Sorry, I've been out cutting alfalfa all afternoon."

"Well…" The word whooshed through the phone as Jacque drew it out. "I'm glad I tried one more time before heading home."

Jennifer returned to the kitchen to check the time. It was later than she'd thought. Where was Cynthia? Shouldn't she be preparing dinner?

"First," Jacque went on, "how is your dad?"

"Progressing. Since his speech came back, we've started having lively phone conversations every night, and some heart-to-heart talks. Although his gait isn't quite normal, he's regained most of the use of his leg. He no longer needs a walker. However—" Jennifer worried a button on her blouse "—his arm and right hand are almost useless." Her voice croaked; she pulled the phone away from her mouth, lifted the cool water to her lips and took a sip.

"That's too bad, but rehabilitation can take a long time."

"I know. Is there something wrong with my column, the magazine layout?"

"I liked your Christmas story, a modern-day retelling of the *Gift of the Magi*. Nice. We're going to run it. The contract's been emailed."

"That's great." Jennifer couldn't stop her wide smile. Finally some good news. "I'll get it signed and back in the mail right away."

"Don't hurry. Since you're on staff, we trust you. Speaking of which, since you worked a beauty theme into the story, we'll run it under your name. But the non-fiction article you pitched, well, we feel it's a conflict of interest. We want you to continue with the article, but you'll have to use a pen name."

A weird feeling shot through Jennifer. "I don't know..."

"Jennifer, you know about branding in the publishing world. When our readers see your byline under the beauty column, they expect something to do with makeup, complexion or hair."

But I'm more than that. Jennifer shook her head to remove the thought. "Wait a minute. By the time the article on the inner-city kids dig runs, I'd be an editor. You can't tell me that the girls read the masthead." She really wanted to use her name for this serious piece.

Dead silence. Had she lost connection? Jennifer pulled the phone away from her ear. Jacque's face still appeared on the screen. "Hello, are you there?"

"Yes." Jacque sighed out the word. "Your name, with this magazine, is branded in beauty. Use your initials and last name. Use your first and middle name. Use an entirely different name. But you can't use Jennifer Edwards."

Was Brett right? She'd hid behind beauty so long that no one would take her seriously?

"So, I need a pen name," Jennifer said. The click of Jacque's keyboard filled the void on the phone. "Do I have to come up with it right now?"

"I don't suppose." Jacque sighed again.

"Is there something else?" Jennifer knew there was. Jacque sighed when she had news to share that might incite confrontation.

"Jennifer, the owner of the magazine is putting pressure on us to fill that editor position because the intern is not working out. I tried to finagle more time, but he wants the editor hired and in position by July first. Quite frankly, I was hoping you'd say that your dad was almost one hundred percent."

Jennifer stumbled backward until her back bumped the wall; then she slid down it. Chin resting on her knees, she drew in a few deep breaths. "So, what exactly are you telling me?"

"The job is yours if you can be back in Chicago by July first."

Running her free hand through her hair, she fisted a wad of her locks, trying to think. "Do you need an answer today?" All of this information was just too much to process at once.

"You know I'm an advocate of family, but this is out of my hands. I will need your answer today because if you turn me down, we have to advertise and interview. And the first of July is fast approaching."

Jennifer wasn't sure if it was the tick of the clock or the beat of her heart that cut through the silent kitchen. There was no way that her dad would be released and home in two weeks. Her chest tightened at the thought of breaking her promise to her dad, and leaving Brett. However, this type of promotion didn't happen every day. She'd worked long hours for six years at the magazine before this position came open. She took another sip of water to clear her throat.

"I'll be there on the first of July."

Chapter 11

Jennifer had hoped a day or two of digging dirt would wear the kids out. She couldn't have been more wrong. They talked over one another at dinner. But they were also a wealth of information. She'd made some mental notes for her article, a good distraction from the secret that weighed on her mind.

Now they scampered around the yard. The first shadows of dusk showing the blink of orange-and-green lightning bugs. The kids ran, hands cupped, hoping to catch one or two of nature's wonders. The adults sat around one of two picnic tables.

"Have you found out any information about the arrowheads, pottery and teeth?" Cynthia leafed through a catalogue selling everything from trinkets to health aides.

"Not the arrowheads. The teeth belong to sheep. The pottery dates back to the early nineteen hundreds. We've found several bottles from that era, too."

Jennifer didn't take her eyes from the children romping toward the knoll. At least she'd be able to stay until their departure.

The crisp page of the catalogue crackled when Cynthia turned it.

Guilt about her decision niggled her mind, and Jennifer only half heard the conversation between Cynthia and Brett.

Eldon lowered the local weekly paper. "I hate to bring up work on a lovely mid-June evening but I'm going to need you to bale the south hay field, Jennifer. I found more rotten fence posts that need to be replaced."

Some of the children looked in their direction when Jennifer released her heavy sigh. "Does it have to be baled tomorrow? I planned to work on my column." *And go watch the kids dig for hands-on research.*

"Yes, it's cured long enough. I'm sorry, but one man fixing a fence takes a while."

Eldon's voice sounded sincere. So Jennifer flashed him a weak smile. "Okay." She could review the readers' questions before she hopped on a tractor, and form the answers in her head while she baled the hay. The short beauty article for November concerned cuticle care. Other than researching new products, she could write that article in her sleep.

She stretched out her arms, splaying her fingers. She should take her own advice. Her short nails were neatly shaped, but she needed a good manicure.

"Why don't you hire a couple of high school boys to help out? I'm guessing they'd work for minimum wage or maybe even by the job." Brett looked from Eldon to Jennifer.

"I don't know. The budget is pretty tight." Suddenly self-conscious about her hands, Jennifer rested them in her lap. Hiring a couple of high school kids might be the answer to her other dilemma.

She planned to keep her secret until the last minute. Although the more she thought about the situation, it started to make her angry. What if her dad's stroke had happened in September instead of April? She would have been the beauty editor by then. They couldn't have demoted or fired her; there were laws against that. Given the years she'd worked for the magazine, you'd think they'd give her the respect she deserved.

"Maybe we should try it." Jennifer ran her hands over her soft denim jeans. "What do you think, Eldon?"

"It'd sure make fixing the fence easier."

Brett nudged Jennifer's arm with his elbow, his touch an instant comfort. "There are a couple of boys at our church who might be interested. Why don't you join me and the kids on Sunday? You can ask them at fellowship. That is, if you can break your rotation."

The look Brett gave her clearly communicated his opinion of her church-hopping ways.

"Someone's coming." Tiffany ran up the grassy knoll.

Wisps of dust from the gravel driveway spiraled in the air before the front of a pickup popped into view.

"The reinforcements are here." Resting his hands on the picnic table, Brett freed his legs from the built-in bench and walked to the driveway to meet his mother. The children gathered around him, curious about the new person on the ranch.

"Marilyn comes out a couple of times every year with treats for the kids." Cynthia closed the wish book.

"Shh." Eldon waved at his wife. "I want to hear what she brought." He twisted his body toward the lane in an effort to hear better.

"He's worse than the kids." Cynthia giggled.

"Who wants homemade ice cream?" Marilyn shouted above the din of chattering.

"What's homemade ice cream?" Rajean pushed on her glasses, and looked up at Brett.

"Ice cream you make at home instead of buying in the store." He tweaked her nose with his index finger.

Jennifer marveled at his camaraderie with the children. He never raised his voice or lost his temper even if he was tired. He made sure each child had something to contribute to the dinner conversations, and defused their rifts with humor.

"Hi, Marilyn." Jennifer scooted over to make room on the bench. "It's really nice of you to bring out homemade ice cream. It's such a special treat."

"Well, it's what I'd do for my grandchildren, if I had some." She shot her son a pointed look.

"Enough of that." Brett gave his mother's stare an evil eye. He placed two grocery sacks on the picnic table and returned to the truck.

Marilyn unpacked nuts, chocolate syrup, caramel and strawberry toppings, plastic spoons and bowls. Metal chinked when Brett dropped the tailgate.

"Eldon, a little help here." Brett slid a round washtub to the end of the tailgate. He flipped two heavy quilts off of it to reveal not one but two stainless steel freezer cans from electric ice cream makers packed in ice.

One on each side, the men hefted the tub to the picnic table.

"Let the serving begin," Brett called in a British accent, slicing a long-handled spoon through the air like it was a scepter.

Cynthia handed out bowls and spoons. The kids stood in line, bowls out in front of them, waiting their turn while Brett served the ice cream. Marilyn assisted with the toppings to make sure the bottles weren't oversqueezed, ruining their dessert.

Taking a head count, Jennifer looked around the yard. "Where's Brandon?" The hazy dusk cast shadows making it difficult to see yet not quite dark enough for the yard lights to click on.

"Last I saw him he was down the knoll by those rocks." Tiffany pulled her spoon from her mouth long enough to talk.

"Brandon," Brett hollered, "come and get some ice cream."

No answer.

"I'll go look for him." Jennifer unfolded herself from the table and headed down the knoll.

"Hey, kids, do you know what kind of vehicle Godzilla drives?" Brett's voice carried over their chatter.

"No, what?" they said, mostly in unison.

Jennifer reached the top of the knoll as Brett delivered the punch line. "A monster truck."

Giggles erupted traveling through the breeze.

"That was a good one," Alex complimented Brett.

Jennifer agreed with him, giggling to herself. She stretched trying to see Brandon's red hair, but dusk's shadow's had settled over of the lower part of the knoll. Stepping around some jagged rocks that jutted from the ground, forming a ledge on the knoll, the rounded toe of her cowboy boots sent loose rock flying under the rocky overhang.

She still didn't see Brandon. She tried to focus farther down the horizon. She saw the white bison calf grazing in the distance but couldn't even make out the shape of the older, darker buffalo. Had Brandon walked clear down the lane to look at the animals?

Giggles tinkled through the air along with something

musical. Maybe maracas? Jennifer smiled. What was Brett up to now?

"Jennifer, we found him. He was in the house," Brett shouted. The children's laughter dying down made the maracas louder. Wanting to get back to the house to see what Brett was up to now, she started to turn to head up the knoll to the main yard.

"Are you guys playing…?" Her mind finally registered what her ears were hearing. Jennifer stopped. The noise from the ice cream social dimming while the rattle magnified. Ever so slowly, Jennifer craned her neck to peek over her shoulder.

Three feet away, in a tight coil, lay a prairie rattler, its rigid tail vibrating a warning. Head erect, mouth open and ready to strike. Fear bolted through her body. The hair on her arms and at the base of her neck stood up. Her pulse thundered in her ears. It took all of her concentration not to run with her body in its fight or flight mode.

"Brett," her voice croaked in a whisper; all the moisture in her mouth had disappeared.

The snake continued its scolding threat with the vibration of its tail.

Sweat trickled down her back and forehead. She must have startled it when she kicked the rock. She opened her mouth, hoping for more volume.

"Brett," her voice squeaked out.

"Jennifer!" Brett hollered her name. He was coming closer.

A little of her panic subsided. He'd rescue her from the vicious rattler.

He's afraid of snakes.

The jarring thought kicked in her adrenaline. She needed to warn him. Holding herself stiff, hoping the rattlesnake hadn't slithered closer, she hollered, "Brett, don't come down here. Keep the kids away."

The vibrations from Brett's footsteps at the top of the knoll scared the snake. The rattles came faster, seemed louder. Her nerves twitched, prickling her skin.

"J-J-Jennifer, don't move."

She heard the fear in his voice. Her own fear ate away at her bones until her body wanted to sag into a heap on the ground. She tried to see if the snake had moved closer, but the frightened tears that burned her eyes, combined with the push of nightfall, made it difficult.

"Brett?" Had he ran for Eldon? Was he frozen with fear above the rocky ledge?

Grass rustled. *Please God, don't let a raccoon scurry out of the tall grass and scare this snake.*

"Jennifer." Brett's voice was soft, yet filled with strength, as it floated through the night. "I need you to listen to me, and to trust me."

A beam of light illuminated the ground around her feet.

"When I say run, go forward six steps and take a hard right." His words were more of a command than instructions. "Can you do that for me?"

"Yes."

"Okay." She heard his ragged breath—or was it hers? Something thumped against the ground behind her.

"Run."

She scrambled forward and to her right, hoping the snake traveled alone. Jennifer hit the loose gravel of the driveway. Her boot soles skidded, sliding her left foot out from under her. She tumbled forward. Gravel bit into her palms. She pushed up, regaining her balance, and kept running.

Something grabbed at her loose shirtsleeve. Rattle-snakes could jump three feet. Had it struck? Were its fangs caught in the fabric of her blouse? She tried to shake her arm, but she felt pressure.

"It's wrapped around my arm," she screamed out into the night. Flinging her arm, she tried to free herself of the snake the way Brett had the day she teased him in the bunkhouse. Then something warm brushed against her shoulders. Was it the snake's tail? How long was this snake?

"Jennifer." The pressure on her arm and grip on her shoulder made her realize someone was running beside her.

"It's me." Brett's breath huffed out. "Stop running."

Stopping, Jennifer sucked in air, her lungs hungry for oxygen.

"Are you okay?" Brett pulled her into a tight embrace. Her cheek to his shoulder, he stroked her hair.

She wrapped her arms around his waist, drawing in his strength. She felt his chest heave, heard his rapid heartbeat.

"Thank you," she whispered. Her tears dampened his shirt, where her head rested.

"I guess I'm always rescuing you." Brett's words came out in huffs.

Jennifer pulled away enough that she could look into his eyes. "Thank God for that." Hoping her shaky legs could hold her, she rose up on her tiptoes and kissed him. She caught the flicker of surprise in his eyes before they fluttered shut.

Her heart rattled with emotion that coiled to the depth of her soul.

Brett ended the kiss and loosened their embrace when a raucous crowd ran down the lane toward them.

A tangle of kid and grownup arms surrounded them in a group hug. The children pushed between them.

"We waited until Eldon gave us the all-clear." Cynthia cupped Jennifer's face with her hands. "Are you all right?"

Jennifer managed to nod her head before Cynthia kissed both of her cheeks. She wiped the tears from Jennifer's face with her thumbs before a tear of her own trickled down her cheek. "When Brett hollered rattler..." Cynthia put a hand to her heart, and shook her head, unable to say any more.

"Mom, Mom."

Brett's raised voice drew everyone's attention. Marilyn had him in a bear hug. "You scared ten years off of my life." She pulled him into her arms. "I am so proud of you." Again, she squeezed him.

"You should have seen him." Jose excitedly hopped on one foot then the other.

"I didn't know anyone could run so fast." Carmen looked dreamily at Brett.

"Or shout so many commands." Carlie giggled. "Eldon seemed to be the only one who understood him at first."

"That's because Brett and I speak the same language when it comes to Jennifer." Eldon pushed through the crowd until he stood in front of her. She braced for another scolding about being too citified, forgetting the rules of ranch life.

He put his hands on her shoulders. His jaw set, he stared into her eyes. "Are you all right?"

"Yes, a little shaken up."

"Me, too." Eldon pulled Jennifer into a fatherly hug. "Because what would I do without you? You are the daughter I never had."

Eldon's show of emotion brought fresh tears to Jennifer's eyes, and guilt to her heart. As quickly as Eldon had embraced her, he let her go, walked over to Brett and shook his hand. "Fast thinking."

"Your dad is going to be so mad he missed this." Marilyn gave Brett another squeeze. Even in the dim nightfall, Jennifer thought she saw a blush spread across his cheeks.

Brett waved his hands at the crew, motioning for them to start walking toward the house. "The excitement's over and the ice cream is melting."

Rajean stood frozen. "You don't think there's another one, do you?"

"I'm sure all your whoops and hollers scared them away." Eldon tweaked her nose and hurried to get into the lead.

Jennifer suspected it was just in case there was another one.

"You should have seen him, Jennifer." Grabbing her arm, Marilyn pushed in between Brett and Jennifer.

"You weren't supposed to see me. I told all of you to stay put. I believe Eldon did, too." The terseness in Brett's voice surprised Jennifer.

The yard lights crackled to life; brightness flooded their path. No longer afraid of what they might be stepping on, the kids raced back to the picnic tables and their melting ice cream.

"Well—" Marilyn raised her eyebrows at Jennifer "—given your history with snakes, Brett, I thought someone should be there to help you."

"Mom." Brett sighed through clenched teeth.

Jennifer stopped walking. Now that her fear had subsided, she tried to turn the event over in her mind. She'd heard a noise, a light thump, and then a harder thump when Brett hollered "Run." She never heard anything after that but her own heartbeat.

"What exactly did happen?"

"It doesn't matter. All that matters is that you're safe." Brett quickened his pace.

"Doesn't matter?" Marilyn scolded. "You faced your fear and a rattlesnake to save Jennifer."

Jennifer stopped. "All I remember is a thumping sound. What did you do?"

Brett turned, hands on his hips. "It's not that big a deal. Let it go, Mom."

Marilyn turned, taking Jennifer's hands in hers. "He threw those heavy quilts on top of the snake, then he jumped down and stood on it while Eldon took care of the snake with a tire tool and you ran away."

"You got that close to a rattlesnake and risked getting bit to save me?" The impact of Brett's actions cut through her foggy mind. She lifted her hand to her heart. Her eyes searched Brett's face. The corner of his mouth curled. Even in the dim light, love shone from his eyes and he nodded.

"It was *nothing*." Brett stressed the last word through clenched teeth, looking at his mother.

"It was romantic." Marilyn sighed.

"It was brave." Jennifer choked out the words around the lump in her throat.

Chapter 12

It was stupid. If he hadn't landed just right so the snake couldn't move, it could have been a disaster. He or Eldon or Jennifer could have been bitten.

He peered through the window of the bunkhouse. A hard rain fell. He yawned and stretched. He'd gotten little sleep between the thunderstorm and his ragged nerves.

He'd let the kids be lazy bugs today and sleep in. Even if it stopped raining, it'd be too muddy at the dig site.

The reel of last night's events played over in his mind. The longer he'd sat at the picnic table the shakier he'd felt inside. His stomach jittered so bad that he'd stopped eating his ice cream. Facing the snake caused only half of his nervous energy.

Jennifer had called out his name. Not Eldon's, not Cynthia's, not Lance's, but his. She could have cried out for help in general, but it was him she'd thought of in her time of need. Him.

Then she'd leaned into his arms.

Stop it, he chided himself. She'd leaned in for comfort because she was scared.

That thought calmed the restless racing of his heart. *She did initiate the kiss and she said I was brave.* His heart was off and running.

A raindrop trickled down the window, leaving an erratic path behind. Brett rested his hands on the window ledge. Leaning toward the glass, he watched the rain and contemplated returning to bed. He'd only gotten about an hour's sleep last night. He remembered checking his phone for what seemed like the millionth time at 3:00 a.m. When a sonic boom of thunder cut through the silence of the night and rattled the bunkhouse windows, it was 4:00 a.m.

It took about an hour to settle the boys back down, and he heard Jennifer doing the same in the girls' bunk. The storm didn't produce lightning, but the deluge of rain that followed lured the children back to sleep, while Brett lay wide-eyed, staring at the wooden planks of the bed frame above him. The same thought played over and over in his mind.

Was it possible that Jennifer cared for him, maybe even loved him? When he told her that he loved her, he hadn't expected anything in return. He'd grown used to the pangs of rejection from her rebuffs when he tried to show his affection for her during high school.

She initiated the kiss. And this isn't high school.

Soft footsteps scuffed across the wooden floor. Jennifer wrapped her arms around his waist. "The alarm didn't go off, so I came out to see why."

Brett lowered an arm to her shoulders, the terry fabric of her robe soft under his fingers. "They can sleep in today. We won't be able to dig. Even if the rain stops it will be too muddy."

The windowpanes framed their reflection, the image of the perfect couple in Brett's mind.

"Thank you again for saving me last night. I guess you're right. You are always rescuing me."

Brett kissed her temple. "You know why."

She shook her head. "I do." Her voice was soft. "I think deep down, I've always known that you loved me. It's why I pushed you away."

She lifted her gaze from the window, her eyes searching his face. His heartbeat pounded with hope yet by the look of turmoil in her eyes, he knew he wasn't going to hear the words he longed for.

"I can't stay here. I'm sorry." The love shining from her eyes was in direct conflict with her words. "I have to go back to Chicago."

"You don't. You're doing everything you do there from here." He stared hard into her eyes. "You could easily commute if you needed to. O'Hare is a major hub."

"You're forgetting about my promotion. The magazine can't have a remote beauty editor." She tipped her head down, averting her eyes to the floor.

Her words rained down on his heart, dampening his hope, like the downpour soaked the ground outside the window.

"Brett, I didn't say I don't have feelings for you but…" Jennifer lifted her eyes to his. The sadness that emanated from them twisted his heart.

"Jennifer and Brett sitting in a tree, k-i-s-s-i-n-g." A chorus of high-pitched giggles followed. The girls tumbled from the door of their room, joining Brett and Jennifer by the window.

A forced smile appeared on Jennifer's face. She turned

toward the girls. "You'd better be good or I'll sic the dogs on you." She lifted one slipper-clad foot, shaking it at them.

More giggles erupted. Joy lit Jennifer's face, which lifted Brett's heart. There had to be some way to make this work. He had faith, but did he have enough faith for both of them?

The adults formed a semicircle around the kitchen island, looking into the living room, where the kids sat in front of the television watching old sitcoms on a satellite station.

Jennifer sipped her coffee. "They can't watch television all day. What are we going to have them do?"

She looked to Brett, who leaned over the opposite end of the island. He shrugged.

"What have you done in previous years?"

"We never experienced a storm of this magnitude while hosting a dig. We'd get a short shower, and go back to work." He lifted his cup to his lips.

"You never had a rainy day plan?"

He shook his head and took a sip of coffee.

"Your magazine's full of ideas for a rainy day," Eldon said. "Why don't you try some?"

Jennifer's mouth gaped. She surveyed the group. No one seemed surprised by Eldon's suggestion. He turned from placing his cup in the sink. "I'm driving down to check on the white buffalo."

"How do you know what *Transitions* publishes?" Jennifer narrowed her eyes, watching him pull a plastic liner over his straw cowboy hat.

Pushing his arm through his slicker sleeve, he called over his shoulder on the way out the door. "I read all the magazines I subscribe to."

Cynthia's guffaws bounced through the house. "You should see your face."

"You subscribe to *Transitions?*"

"Not me. Eldon. Matthew, too. The day it arrives, we clear our evening and read through it together. The beauty advice column first, of course."

Emotion clogged Jennifer's throat. "I had no idea."

"We didn't forget you when you moved to Chicago." Cynthia sobered.

Her words cut through Jennifer, laying her heart flat, like fallen alfalfa after running a swath through the field. She had left her home without looking back. Isn't that what she planned to do again?

"Well, I'm open to suggestions. We could have a movie marathon." Brett spun his empty cup around by the handle, antsier than the kids.

"The magazine does focus on girls—" Jennifer rubbed her lips together, savoring the coffee flavor that lingered there "—so I'm not sure if any of my suggestions will work for the boys."

"True." Cynthia nodded. "You suggest arts and crafts for the girls that the boys might not enjoy."

Brett sighed.

"I think we're okay for now." Jennifer snatched the coffeepot from its perch, silently offering to pour. "They seem to enjoy this sitcom even if it is in black-and-white, so we can brainstorm for a while." She topped off everyone's cup and returned the pot to the heat element. She hoped the caffeine kicked in soon to ease her lack of sleep.

"We could have a board game competition? Are my games still on the top shelf of the hall closet?" Jennifer turned to Cynthia.

"They are. Maybe they could write letters home or thank-you notes to the sponsors."

"The last one is a good idea, Cynthia. They need to do that, anyway." Brett scrubbed his face with his hands. He seemed to be having the same trouble staying alert, too. He hadn't shaved or tucked his pocketed red T-shirt into his jeans this morning, giving him a disheveled look that she found very appealing.

The hinges of the back door squeaked open, and a cool breeze laced with the pungent smell of soggy ground accompanied Eldon into the kitchen. A second set of footsteps sounded on the tile floor of the mudroom.

"Special delivery for Jennifer Edwards." Lance flashed his familiar smile, pushing a cardboard box across the island countertop.

He patted Brett's back when he passed by him. "Heard you're a hero."

The set of Brett's jaw, accompanied by the sideways glance he gave Lance, was a warning that he wasn't in the mood to be needled today.

"What?" Lance met Brett's warning glare. "I'm glad you saved her. She's my blood sister." Lance held up an index finger, a visible scar on the pad. "All brothers treat the guys who show interest in their sisters this way."

Brett blinked his eyes in disbelief. "All this time…" He looked from Lance to Jennifer.

"I had no idea he was showing brotherly love."

Jennifer rubbed her thumb over her index finger, feeling the slight bump of a scar, remembering the day they realized they'd never have siblings of their own, and made their childhood pact.

"Don't tell me you didn't know that, bro." Lance took a swig of coffee.

Sheepishness washed the anger from Brett's face. "I guess I didn't put it together."

A soft click drew Jennifer's attention away from the

conversation. The laundry room door now closed, Eldon and Cynthia made their silent escape.

"Everyone in Faith knew you liked Jennifer—" Lance jerked his head toward Jennifer "—except Jennifer. I had to make sure you respected her, and treated her well."

The door in her heart that she'd locked twelve years ago sprang open. She'd known Brett had had feelings for her but couldn't let that get in the way of her escape from Faith, and a chance to pursue her dreams. It was easier to fight with Brett than return his feelings. If she'd have given in to her emotions, she'd have stayed in Faith, possibly never turning her dream of being a journalist into a reality.

Her eyes widened. She stared into the dark brew in her cup, seeing Brett's eye color. It was part of the reason she felt guilty now. She shouldn't have allowed herself to show her love for him; she'd worked so hard for that promotion. She had to go back to Chicago, didn't she? How could she have a career here?

"Anyway—" Lance held out his hand to Brett. "I owe you an apology. I knew you'd never hurt Jennifer when I saw you in the back of the sheriff's car and when you didn't tell them who the spray paint really belonged to. I'm sorry I let you go through that and didn't come forward to tell the truth."

The surreal happenings that had begun last night when she'd startled a snake made Jennifer's head spin. Had she heard an apology from Lance? Were he and Brett really shaking hands?

"I did it for Jennifer, you know. She would have hated me if I'd turned you in," Brett said matter-of-factly.

"I know." Lance placed his free hand over their clenched hands. "No hard feelings?"

"No hard feelings."

For the first time in her life, Jennifer saw Brett smile at Lance.

"Jennifer." Lance moved until he stood in front of her. "I know you think I should apologize to you. I told you to stay inside the gym, yet you followed us outside. None of this would have happened if you'd have listened to me."

Anger sprung inside of her. Would she never get the apology that she deserved? "What? Now you're going to blame me?" In a split second her anger died. Isn't that what brothers and sisters did, blame each other? He *had* told her that she couldn't hang around him and his friends that night.

She smiled at him, and watched a wide smile cross his face.

"I am sorry that I pushed the aerosol can into your hands. I panicked. I put on a good show of bravado in my teenage years, but I wasn't really brave." He hitched a thumb over his shoulder. "Not the way this guy was."

"He was brave last night." Carmen's dreamy voice danced through the kitchen.

"That's what I hear." Lance smiled at Brett.

"The episode is over. A different show is on." Carmen shook her head, wrinkling her nose. She rested her elbows on the table, placing her chin in her hands. "Now what are we going to do?" Her dreary tone rivaled the gray clouds hovering close to the ground outside of the window.

"It's a good day for another Monopoly match." Alex sauntered into the room. Rajean, right behind him, almost stepped on the backs of his heels.

She wrinkled her nose. "I don't want to play that game. What's in the box?" She picked at a loose piece of cardboard not covered with packing tape.

Jennifer glanced at the address label. "Beauty products from the *Transitions* office."

"Can I see what's inside?" She stood on her tiptoes, eyes even with the box's top.

"Sure."

"I'll go get the other girls." Rajean ran out of the kitchen, hollering all the way.

In seconds the excited girls pushed Lance and Brett out of their way to see what was inside.

"This is my cue to go back down and make sure Faith and her mom are okay." Lance started for the door.

"You named my white buffalo calf?" Jennifer inflected annoyance on purpose.

Lance turned and shrugged. "You snooze, you lose, sis."

"Faith—" Jennifer smiled "—is perfect."

Lance rapped on the laundry room door. "You two can come out now." He winked at Jennifer. "I need a ride back down the lane."

The door creaked open and Cynthia peeked out. Her eyes went from Lance to Brett to Jennifer; then her wide smile creased her face. "It's about time."

"Let's go, son." Eldon put his cowboy hat on his head.

"So what do you think it is?" Tiffany danced from foot to foot.

"I never know what products the sponsors are going to send." Jennifer's expression was full of wonder, matching the girls.

She looks good surrounded by children. Brett drank in the moment, allowing a self-indulgent daydream of what their children might look like.

The packing tape purred its release under Jennifer's quick jerk. The box flaps popped open a few inches. Four sets of eyes tried to peek through the narrow opening before Jennifer flipped the cardboard flaps back, opening the box to bare its contents. She removed air-filled packing pillows.

"It's products for a manicure." Jennifer pulled out a bottle of bright green nail polish. The girls exclaimed that it was the prettiest color they'd ever seen, until Jennifer produced a purple-colored bottle.

Brett shook his head. "Who would want purple nails?"

All of the females looked at him. "It's lilac," their voices chorused, their faces aghast at his mistake. Jennifer's eye roll, reminiscent of their youth, irked him a little. His mouth set in a grim line.

"Brett, come and help me get those board games from the top shelf of the hall closet."

Cynthia zigzagged through the group of girls surrounding the kitchen isle and looking into the cardboard box like it contained the mysteries of life. Jennifer pulled out a rounded bottle filled with bright pink liquid.

"Ladies, these are the colors that will be popular in the spring." The thrill of excitement in Jennifer's voice didn't escape him.

The happy giggles of the girls trailed him into the hallway, where Cynthia waited by the closet.

He didn't get it. Why would a girl want purple or green fingernails?

Arms loaded with board games in various-size boxes, he and Cynthia returned to the kitchen.

"Come on, everyone, let's play. We can play with teams, boys against girls." Brett eased the games he held onto the island.

"Jennifer's going to teach us how to do manicures." Carmen carefully carried a small bowl filled with water to the table.

"I thought it'd be a good way for them to pass the afternoon." Jennifer laid a paper towel square in front of each of the girls sitting around the table.

"Will you write about this in your column?" Tiffany rolled some type of utensil in her fingers.

"What a good idea! I can do a step-by-step how-to-article." Jennifer patted Tiffany's head.

Brett opened his mouth to argue that this was supposed to be an educational experience for the girls.

"You children inspire my creativity. I'm writing a piece on your dig, that my editor will publish in an upcoming issue." Jennifer laid all the products she'd removed from the box in an orderly row.

"What?" Brett perked up at this information. Jennifer looked at him, smiling.

"An old friend reminded me of my former writing talents. *Transitions* accepted a short story for their Christmas issue, and the nonfiction article on your dig that I proposed."

The pleased look on her face said she expected a positive response, which he could have done had she not mentioned the nonfiction article. Is that what all the questions were about the other night? He'd thought she was actually taking an interest in him and his work. Foolish disappointment crept through him. Had she been using him?

After a few seconds of silence, Jennifer drew her brows together and turned her attention to the table. "Girls, we'll do one hand at a time, so place the fingers of your dominant hand in the bowls."

Once the girls' fingers were soaking, Jennifer walked over to him. She kept her voice low. "I thought you'd be happy that I used my talent for something other than makeup." Her eyes searched his face.

"I am but…" Brett looked over her head to the table of

girls chattering away. "We'll have to talk about that later. Go on back to your rainy-day activity."

After Brett set up card tables in the living room, and the boys got started playing games, he returned to the kitchen. He leaned against the door frame, watching Jennifer explain the manicure tools and that a manicure was more than painting their nails, it was an essential part of hygiene.

"I have a question." Rajean's bubbly voice grew soft and serious.

"What is it?" Jennifer stopped what she was doing to her own nails.

Rajean hung her head. "It's not about nails." Her voice was a whisper.

From his sideways advantage, he saw her eyes lift, looking over her glasses. "How do I tell my dad that I need to use deodorant? I've been sneaking some of his, but then I smell like a boy." Red spots blotched her cheeks.

"Why don't you ask your mom?" Carmen looked up from her concentrated efforts.

"I don't know my mom." Rajean's eyes were now downcast.

"I didn't, either." Jennifer reached out and squeezed Rajean's arm. "Sometimes it's hard to ask a dad something so personal, isn't it?"

Rajean nodded.

"My mom lives in another state." Carlie stopped what she was doing. "I have a stepmom though, and I can ask her that kind of stuff. Did you have a stepmom?"

"I had Cynthia, but it was Brett's mom that helped me the most with girl stuff. I'd see her on the street or at school or somewhere and she—" a wistful look crossed Jennifer's face "—just seemed to know my questions before I asked them. She'd invite me to her house for a treat.

We'd be talking and she'd bring up the subject in everyday conversation, giving me a chance to ask my questions."

Realization reeled through Brett, making him dizzy.

"That's what you do in your beauty advice column, only with makeup, not hygiene." Tiffany ran an emery board across her nails.

"Hmm." Jennifer rubbed her lips together, an inspired look on her face. "Rajean, do you have an aunt or a friend or someone you can talk to?"

"My grandma, I guess." Rajean resumed her normal posture.

"You should cover this kind of stuff in your column. If we all write letters to you, will you answer them?" Tiffany's wide eyes held excitement.

"I would."

"We'll be famous with our names in *Transitions*."

A fit of giggles filled the room, and a new respect for his mother and Jennifer filled Brett's heart. He'd been wrong. Makeup and beauty advice wasn't fluff. Beauty for women went far beyond the colors they wore on their faces. His mother's beauty filled a void in a little girl's life in an unobtrusive way. Jennifer, in her own way, was doing the same thing.

The sharing of questions and answers continued. Pride shined from Jennifer's beautiful blue eyes. If she was promoted to beauty editor, she could add articles about hygiene to answer shy little girls' questions. She reached thousands of girls every month, answering their most personal inquiries. Her work was meaningful and had immediate results in some girls' lives. Now that he realized the importance of her work, he could never ask her to give it up.

Chapter 13

Brett walked behind the kids, watching them carefully dig and study the rocks they uncovered. He'd moved them to a location shaded by the cliffs. Although the ground remained soggy from yesterday's rain, it protected the children from the glaring midafternoon sunshine.

So far, the dig had been successful during the course of their stay. They'd found a few fossils, a lot of rose quartz and a few bones. The fossils and rocks, they'd get to take home. The bones would be specimens for study at the university. The bones belonged to a small animal, probably the leftovers of a coyote's dinner, perhaps a sheep. They were old but not prehistoric; he could tell that by looking at them. After further study under a microscope, he'd identify them.

The rain-soaked ground forced the kids to dig deeper into the soil, which seemed to take less concentration and created more chatter on their success or failure to find something. Their silly conversations on what they would uncover widened his smile. The faith of a child, always believing in possibilities.

The whine of an ATV slowing down drew his attention to the path leading into the rocky crags where the children dug. Jennifer waved after she stopped the vehicle and dismounted. She unhooked a cooler from the back, slung a camera case over her shoulder and headed toward him.

A bright smile lit her face. She marched through the stubby grass toward the digging crew. Her dark denim jeans were a contrast to the light blue chambray shirt she wore like a jacket over a turquoise T-shirt, all blue but no match for her dazzling sky-colored eyes that twinkled with happiness.

"Not taking any chances?" Brett tipped his head toward her high-stepping feet.

Her laugh rippled off of the rocks, and bounced through the valley. "Not for a while. I brought some juice boxes and oranges. I thought the kids might need some hydration."

Brett relieved her of the cooler, stashing it on a rock shelf.

"I found something." Brandon tapped his digging tool on his find. The clink of metal hitting metal resounded around them.

Brett hurried over to the area where he dug, and shined a flashlight into the one-foot hole Brandon had dug straight down.

"What do you think it is?" Brandon rubbed his cheek, leaving a smudge of mud behind.

"I can't tell, but let's get this hole wider. Jennifer, will you bring me one of those shovels?" Brett pointed to several leaning against the bluff. "I'll break up the ground a little more. Then we'll work together so we can see what Brandon found."

Jennifer brought the shovel. Cupping her eyes, she peered down into the hole with the children.

"Okay, everyone will have to move back. I'm going to make a rectangle about two feet by three feet. Whatever Brandon found is down pretty far, so I'll lift about a foot of topsoil off before you can dig. Why don't you take a break, and have some treats that Jennifer brought?"

The kids ran over to the cooler.

"There are sanitary hand wipes in the cooler. Use those before you break into the food," Jennifer called after the anxious children.

Jennifer slipped her camera from the case around her shoulder. "I need to snap some pictures of this for my article."

A hard breath puffed out of Brett when he heaved the shovel into the ground, bending the handle back. A triangle of wet soil popped up with the sharp shovel blade. Brett frowned, inserting the shovel, and then repeated the previous procedure. "How is this article going to fit in your beauty advice? Wait, I know—make your own mud pack." Panic shot through Brett at his last statement. He hadn't meant to make fun of Jennifer's occupation. There was a void that her beauty advice filled, he knew that now. He was just so used to turning the kids' words around and making them into puns.

He chanced a glance at Jennifer. Her mouth puckered and pulled to the side.

"Very funny, Professor Lange," she said before a wide smile broke across her face. "Actually, like I told you before, it's an article about girls and archeology. The magazine does cover more than fashion and beauty, you know."

"I know." Brett squared a corner and turned. "They

have a department about various occupations. Is this where this article will go?"

"How do you know that?" Jennifer crossed her arms and stared hard in his direction.

"I don't subscribe, if that's what you're thinking." Brett stopped digging. Swiping the sweat on his brow, he bumped back his fedora to expose his forehead. "Mom does. I might have picked it up and read it once or twice."

A soft look settled on Jennifer's face, pleased that he'd read the magazine.

"So, why are you writing an article on this?"

"Someone reminded me that I used to write more than 'fluff.'" Jennifer air quoted her last word with her fingers. "But I need pictures to go with the article. So do you mind if I take a few at various stages? The problem is I'd need a photo release for the girls, so I plan to take them of the area, and the digging process."

Brett nodded and stepped back, while Jennifer took pictures from various angles.

"What do you think is down there?"

"My guess, looking at the raised nub of metal, is a horseshoe. Which makes sense, because the graduate students found a branding iron on the other side of the rocks by the foundation. I think there must have been a barn or line camp or something here at one time."

"Really?" Jennifer looked around. "It's always been dirt and rocks since I can remember."

"Yeah, me, too. Beautiful dirt and rocks." Brett sighed, raking topsoil from the square he'd created. Growing up, he would have given anything to live on this ranch instead of in town. Really, he still would, but it was way too long a commute.

Jennifer snapped another picture.

"Okay, let's dig," Brett hollered to his digging crew,

then watched them scramble from the rocky ledge they'd climbed.

It didn't take long for the eight kids to uncover Brandon's treasure, although Brett had to remind them several times to be careful so they didn't damage whatever time had buried under the soil and rock.

Brandon dropped his tool; using his hand, he pulled his find free. He held it up in the air.

"What is it?" Rajean stopped digging.

Brandon shrugged.

"A horseshoe." Alex glanced back into the dirt. "Think there's any more?"

"I don't know. We still have some time before dinner. You can keep digging if you'd like."

"How do you think that got there?" Carmen stabbed at the dirt with her tool, obviously hoping to hit something metal.

"Some horse probably lost it." Carlie looked over Brandon's shoulder.

Brett stifled a laugh, noticing Jennifer was doing the same.

"But how?" Brandon held the horseshoe in the air. Turning it back and forth he studied it from all angles.

Pulling a plastic bag from his pocket, Brett held it open. Brandon dropped his find into it. Brett zipped it shut. "I'll analyze this and let you know how old it is. In the meantime, when you get home you should visit the library or search the internet and see if you can determine the era it came from."

"How will we remember what it looks like?" Rajean pushed her glasses up her nose.

"I'll take a picture and Brett will mail or email it to you." Jennifer held up her camera.

"Excellent idea." Brett nodded to Jennifer. "You can use a picture of that in your article, too."

"I bet it fell off of a general's horse during the war." Jose sat back on his heels.

"Or maybe a chief's horse," Tiffany added.

"I don't think Native people shoed their horses," Alex interjected. "But a wagon train might have gone through and lost one."

Brett moved closer to Jennifer, inhaling the fresh scent of her perfume. "Quite a bit of speculating going on," Brett whispered in a conspiratorial tone. Then he grinned. "I think it's from the early nineteen hundreds. Time will tell, though." He motioned toward the crags with his head. "Shall we go over here and you can snap a few shots?"

Brett placed his hand on the small of Jennifer's back, guiding her toward the edge of the rock formation where she'd left the ATV.

"Do you mind if I read your article before you send it off?"

"That would be great, because I need a few quotes from an expert."

A thrill shot through him at Jennifer's remark. Between the article and her request, she respected his work. "I'd be honored." Brett dipped into a small bow. "I'm also glad that you are expanding your writing."

"Because you don't like fluff?"

Brett winced. "That was before I saw you working with the girls on their manicures and heard their questions." He adjusted his hat. "You were right, Jennifer. I did have a charmed life compared to a lot of kids."

"Well, it's all you knew growing up here."

"I guess. What I mean is you are already a talented writer. I'm glad you are trying another type of writing."

Brett expected Jennifer's face to brighten from his compliment; instead, her face grew serious.

"You know, they won't let me run this article under my real name."

"Why?"

"Jacque's excuse was that readers would see my name and expect beauty to be a part of the article." Her exhalation came out in a huff.

"You disagree."

"I do. I don't think kids would care."

"Then tell them you want it under your real name or you'll sell it to someone else."

Jennifer's face brightened. "You know, I did research other magazine markets after she told me that, but the slant on the article fits with *Transitions* guidelines, and I did offer it to her first, so I'll use another name."

"What are you going to use?"

"Jacque suggested my middle name and last name, but…" She kicked at an imaginary rock with the toe of her boot.

"That was your mom's name, right?"

"Yes, and although it'd be nice to honor her, I don't really want to be known as her, either." Jennifer sighed.

"Use her maiden name."

"That's an idea, I guess." Jennifer shrugged. "Look, I'd better get back and see if Cynthia or Eldon need any help."

She took a step to leave, then shot him an apprehensive glance. He didn't miss his cue; he had about fifteen years to make up for. He caught her arm, stopping her, and then leaned down and gave her a chaste goodbye kiss.

As he watched her slender form walk back toward the ATV, the breeze gently catching the loose tails of her shirt, he knew a way Jennifer could use a different name and her real name on that article. He'd played the scenario around in his head for years. It'd be a dream come true for him, yet he couldn't ask her to give up her promotion, not after he understood the importance of her work.

Faith was no longer his home, but when he hungered for the beauty of nature or the adventure of finding a fossil, the country was a short drive out of Rapid City. He rested his hand on his hips, looking at the vastness of the land, the glorious rocks and the horizon line where the sky met the earth. Could he leave this behind and live in Chicago?

From a distance, Jennifer could see Eldon working on the fence line. She angled the ATV in his direction, bumping over the uneven pasture ground.

Cutting the engine, she threw her leg over the seat and slid off. "Want some help?"

"Not work for girls." Eldon shook his head, wrapping barbed wire around a new fence post and then driving a nail in to secure it. "Might ruin their citified nails." He peered up under his straw cowboy hat and winked.

"I've burned that bridge." Jennifer splayed her fingers, the petal-pink polish from yesterday already chipped. She turned her hand to show him.

"Don't you have a column to write?" Eldon hammered in another staple nail.

"My deadline for the next one isn't for a week, so I have some time if you need help."

"Well, hold the post steady, and I'll fill in some dirt. I didn't wait until Sunday. I called those two boys from Brett's church. They are coming out to help with this tomorrow. Are you sure we can afford it?"

"The bank extended our line of credit after I gave them an accurate head count of the cattle and buffalo herds. They'll use them as collateral until we take them to the livestock auction barn in town." Jennifer tamped some dirt Eldon placed around the hole with her boot.

"We had a good spring." Eldon stomped the dirt on his side.

"Yes, we did. We didn't lose a single calf to sickness or predators. Think Dad is proud of me?"

Eldon stopped what he was doing. "Your dad has always been proud of you. We all have."

Jennifer's heart expanded at Eldon's statement, tears welling in her eyes.

"I spoke to the doctor, and he isn't hopeful that Dad will regain the full use of his right hand."

"I know. Matthew told Cynthia and me when we went to see him earlier this week. He's pretty good at using his left hand for some things, but…" Eldon stared off into the horizon, shaking his head, sadness in his eyes, a slight frown on his lips. Jennifer knew he shared the same concern, and love when it came to her dad.

"If I don't go back to Chicago by July first, they're giving my promotion to someone else," she blurted.

Eldon's brown eyes rested on her face. She saw understanding even though he huffed. "Maybe one of these boys will work out part-time."

"Maybe." Jennifer looked over her shoulder. She liked what she was doing, especially now that she'd met girls who read her column and benefited from it. But she wasn't sure she wanted to be beauty editor anymore. What would happen if she stayed here? Would they let her continue in the beauty columnist position?

"Your heart says stay."

Jennifer turned to face Eldon and nodded. "For more reasons than what you think."

"You should follow you heart."

"I know, but…"

"You want a sign?"

Jennifer shook her head, and smiled. "No, I don't need a sign." For this decision, she'd rely on faith.

Chapter 14

Sunday lived up to its name; glistening beams of sunlight filtered through the mini blinds casting stripes on the decades-old paint covering the walls of her childhood bedroom. Jennifer sighed. A little piece of her heart hated to say goodbye to her room. But what else could she do? She had to go back to Chicago.

The thought made her heart hang heavy in her chest. Chicago didn't hold the same appeal it had nine weeks ago. It was nice to go into town where people greeted you by name. It was nice to share supper every night with people that she loved. It was nice to be home.

She gave one last glance at her image in the vanity mirror. The colorful wraparound dress, paired with white strappy flats, screamed fashionable, yet was cool and comfortable in the late June heat. She dabbed a new hair product on her fingers before fluffing up her hair. Applied to the hairline, the product produced height and body. Applied to the ends of the hair, it helped to sculpt. Jennifer twisted and pulled until her short locks framed her face in a flattering way.

For her finishing touch, she brushed powder across her face. She splayed her fingers. Her manicured nails sported a clear coat of polish. Finding a few extra minutes earlier in the morning, she'd treated herself and polished her nails. She opened her bedroom door. Muffled giggles and guffaws echoed down the hall.

"Tell us another one," Jose coaxed.

"Do you know why the skeleton wouldn't cross the road?" Brett used a funny voice.

Jennifer entered the kitchen. Brett's raised brows were barely visible under a mass of brown curls coiled on his forehead. He looked at each child for some type of response.

"We don't know," Jose finally answered.

"He had no guts."

Jennifer cringed, but the kids burst out laughing, right along with the joke teller.

Brett's sun-kissed face and neck set off the white polo shirt he wore tucked into khaki trousers with a deep crease. His light brown leather loafers gave his Sunday best a polished look.

"We're ready to go." Brett motioned toward the door.

All of the kids tumbled through the door and into the van calling dibs on various seats. The silly joke-telling didn't stop until Brett pulled into the church's parking lot.

"Hope Mom saved enough seats." Brett held the passenger door open. Jennifer slipped from the seat.

"Thank you." She smiled at him, breathing in his spicy cologne.

The kids gathered around them, helping them greet neighbors while entering the church.

Marilyn waved to them from the front of the church. The usher met their group, leading them to a long pew. Marilyn sat on the isle end of the pew, then the four girls. Jennifer sat in the middle of the pew, with Brett to her left. Brett's dad anchored the opposite end of the pew, sandwiching the boys between him and Brett. The adults exchanged confident smiles that the seating arrangement would help them manage any antics during the service.

Of all the churches Jennifer attended in Faith, this was her favorite with its oval-shaped windows depicting stained-glass images of Christ. Spiral stairs led to the choir loft and the rich brown oak alter. Her parents had been married in front of that alter. A short two years later, after her mother died in childbirth, her casket had stood there during her memorial service. The thought used to disturb Jennifer, remind her that she didn't have a family. But today, sitting in the pew with Brett and his family, the thought of having roots in a church brought her comfort.

God hadn't abandoned her. She'd been too young to understand. Cynthia, Marilyn and many other women in town had tried to fill the void for her. In that second, joy burst through Jennifer's heart. She hadn't been *pitied*, she'd been *loved*. She'd never had the faith to see it before.

Jennifer turned misty eyes to Brett and smiled. He wrinkled his forehead and squinted. He pulled a face before resting his palm over her hand. A giggle bubbled in Jennifer at the puzzlement on his face. She managed to swallow the sound with a small hiccup.

The service didn't suffer too many interruptions from the rowdy group. Before she knew it, they were shaking hands with the minister at the door.

"Would you like to walk to Mom and Dad's with me? Dad agreed to drive the van with the kids to their house."

"Sure." Jennifer's heart lifted at the look in Brett's eyes.

He gave the thumbs-up sign to his dad, then slipped his hand in hers and turned down the sidewalk that looped the long way to his parents' house, their hands gently swinging between them.

"You know, that is my favorite church in Faith."

"It's the only one I know. Other than funerals, I've never attended worship anywhere else in Faith. Why is it your favorite?"

"It's my family's church."

The same puzzled look Brett had worn in church returned. Jennifer released a giggle. "Don't look so amazed. My mom and dad married there. My mom's funeral was there. Dad stopped going after that."

"Why all the rotation to the other churches?" Brett's questioning tone matched the look on his face.

Jennifer shrugged, breaking the rhythm of their arm swinging. "Curiosity, I guess. Maybe a search for answers. The various denominations' worship services are so different in their delivery of the word of God, yet all their messages are the same. Jesus is our friend and savior. If we trust him with our lives, things will work out."

Brett laughed.

Jennifer drew her brows together. "What?" She turned to look at him.

He stared down the street. "Sorry, it's nothing really."

"It *is* something." Jennifer broke free of Brett's grasp, moving so she could face him. "You always give me a look, or make a noise, when I pray, or talk about God. Do you think I'm not a believer, that I don't have religion?"

Brett placed his hands on his hips, one knee bent the other straight. "No, I believe that you are religious, but what you described is faith, and quite frankly, Jennifer, you don't have it."

"Oh, and you, a scientist, know so much about faith?" Ire tinged her voice.

"My work is all about faith. I dig in dirt hoping to uncover something. Even though I can't look down and see it, I believe it's there so I work to uncover it. Look at Sue T-Rex. It'd been in that rock for a long time; it took the faith of one person to uncover it."

"You're using a dinosaur as an example of faith?"

"You asked for a sign to make sure everything would return to normal, *your* normal, instead of trusting God. Yet you know what faith is. You just described it." Brett lifted his hand and cupped her cheek. "Look, I don't want to argue about this."

His brown eyes held the sincerity that sounded in his words. Yet his opinions of her chafed her heart. First she was shallow, now lacking faith. How on earth could she love this man when it seemed his favorite thing to do was point out her faults?

Jennifer's breath caught in her chest. Her eyes rounded.

"Are you okay?" Brett stared at her hard. "You're pale and you look scared."

Her heart hammered in her chest. Was it because her thoughts frightened her a little bit or because of his touch?

"We need to get to your parents. They'll be worried."

"Jennifer, tell me what's wrong."

"You gave me something to think about, that's all. I did ask for a sign, I can't argue with you there." She backed away from him, turned on her heel and hurried down the sidewalk, the insoles of her sandals snapping on her heels with each step.

The quick clicks sounding on the cement behind her were an indication that Brett was catching up to her. He was right. She knew it. She didn't have faith that everything would work out. She wanted a sign from God that said "everything will go back to normal." But it wouldn't. Even if her dad fully recovered and she went back to her promotion in Chicago, nothing would be the same for her. Her heart would break with her unspoken love for Brett. If she declared her love for him, and then left, that would be cruel. Crueler than anything else she'd done to him throughout their lives.

Salty tears pooled in her eyes, burning them until she blinked. The tears weren't caused by Brett's words but by the realization that God was working out the situation in His way. Nothing would be the same. Brett put too many thoughts in her head, telling her she was more than fluff until she believed him and wrote a fiction and nonfiction article for the magazine. Telling her that she knew what faith was but didn't apply it to her life. She'd asked for a sign from God, and she'd gotten it in the form of a white buffalo calf.

Cynthia's words popped into her mind. "A sign of well-being on the verge of an awakening. I was talking about you."

Jennifer came to the crosswalk on Main Street. Her breath came fast as she realized she was at a crossroads in her life. She stopped and spun around. Brett hovered behind her, the way he always had, a quiet reassurance that someone was watching her back. Loving her. How many times had he proved that? How many times did he have to prove that?

She swiped at the tears with her fingers.

He stepped toward her, pulled her into his arms. "I'm sorry I mentioned it. I don't know what it is about you that makes me always say the wrong thing, do the wrong thing."

Jennifer pulled her head back, narrowing her eyes at him. "I hope you don't think that you did the wrong thing the other night when you saved me. Or said the wrong thing when you told me that you loved me?"

"I think those are the only right things I've ever done for you." His wistful tone and sad expression swelled Jennifer's heart. The same heart Eldon had advised her to follow.

The joy bursting inside of her brought a smile to her lips. "That's not true." Men made grand gestures all the time for women. Why couldn't women do the same? Jennifer pushed free of Brett's embrace and grabbed him by the hand. This was the time of day on Sunday that most of the church services ended and traffic picked up in the small community. She let a pickup pass, returning their wave before she pulled Brett out into the center of the street.

"What are you doing?"

A car whizzed past, honking the horn.

Jennifer giggled.

Brett pulled on her arm. "Let's get out of the middle of the street."

Firming her stance, she shook her head. Brett put his hands on his hips, with one knee bent. His look of confusion brought another giggle to Jennifer's lips. A giggle she'd decided to share, so she sauntered up to him, wrapped her arms around his neck and kissed him, in broad daylight for all of Faith to see.

"That was to thank you for the time you rescued me in high school." She puckered up and found her mark again. This time his soft lips yielded to hers, his hands resting on her shoulders. "That kiss was for conquering your fear of snakes to save me from being bitten. And this one—"

Jennifer leaned toward Brett, but his lips found hers first, and took control of the kiss.

He wrapped his arms around her, and ended the kiss

the moment her knees went weak. "And what was that one for?"

"Because I love you, Brett Lange."

A small look of disbelief flickered in Brett's eyes before his lips curled into that apprehensive grin that she wanted to kiss right off of his face. But that could wait—right now she was happy losing herself in his beautiful brown eyes.

"I love you, too." Brett narrowed his eyes. "But now the whole town knows."

"I think they always did." Jennifer's laugh rang out like church bells announcing Sunday service.

Brett nodded before resting his forehead against hers and nuzzling her nose with his. "Do you love me enough to marry me?" He released his embrace and, holding on to her left hand, he dropped to one knee. "I don't have a ring to offer you at this moment, but I can offer you all the love in my heart. Jennifer, would you marry me?"

Jennifer's heart jackhammered its response to the depth of love shining from Brett's brown eyes.

"Yes." The word sighed from her, floating through the main street of town.

Brett squeezed her hand, stood and wrapped her in a tight embrace.

A few cars swerved around them, honking their horns in a repeating pattern, the way small-town people acknowledge their friends and neighbors. One car stopped beside them and the window purred down.

"That was so romantic!" Marilyn waved her arm, her bangle bracelets clamoring together. "Does this mean there is still hope for grandchildren?"

Jennifer splayed her fingers. Her day-old French manicure paled in comparison to the sparkling of the diamonds in her wedding band. She smiled. Standing on the porch of the bunkhouse, she wiggled her finger. The jewels' facets caught the sun and sent their dazzle back into the sky. The soft click of the door gently closing behind her broke her fascination with their symbol of love.

"Mrs. Lange."

A pleasant shiver tickled through Jennifer when Brett's warm breath bounced against the sensitive skin of her neck. Turning her head, their gazes locked. The love shining from his brown eyes more brilliant than her princess-cut diamond.

"Are you ready to go to the reception?"

"Not quite." The late-afternoon ceremony at the church in Faith had been beautiful but hectic with the bride and groom being pulled in different directions since sun-up. Jennifer was glad for the quiet hour she'd scheduled on their wedding day to enjoy each other as man and wife.

Brett ran his hand down her arm until his grasp found hers. He lifted it to his lips, then moved down a step. "They're waiting."

She nodded, admiring her handsome husband's broad shoulders in his Western-cut black tuxedo. His black cowboy boots had been buffed to a high shine. He'd wanted to wear the traditional shiny shoes until they'd decided the location of the reception. Practically had won out, and he'd gone with leather boots.

But then so had she. Who knew what lurked in one of the rocky crags by the dig site? She'd learned her lesson. The white lace-up boots she wore rested four inches above her ankle. The pointed toe gave them a Western feel, yet the five-inch heels screamed fashion. Eldon had shaken his head when he saw the citified shoes, but Brett's raised eyebrows and appreciative grin had sent a thrill through her, reinforcing her choice of footwear.

"I have something for you." Jennifer pulled her hand free and slipped into their weekend honeymoon bungalow, the bunkhouse. A few seconds later, Brett waited at the bottom of the stairs, offering her his hand to assist her. She tucked the gift under her arm, and lifted the gored satin skirt of her mother's wedding gown, pleased that her dad had kept it all these years.

Her tailor in Chicago had marveled at her mother's sewing skills on the popular Simplicity pattern. The tailor even knew the pattern number. Not many adjustments had needed to be made—a little tucking to adjust the bodice to set above her normal waistline. The Chantilly lace cape collar formed short flared cap sleeves. The high neckline made accessorizing unnecessary. A trio of delicate pearls dropped from her ears. Satin and lace ribbons, with embedded pearls, entwined in a weave that covered her veil cap. The short tulle veil, which had covered her face during the ceremony, was now removed from the headpiece. Clasping Brett's fingers in her hand, she carefully walked down the steps.

"You are beautiful." Brett pulled her into an embrace. His lips claimed a tender kiss.

"Thank you," Jennifer whispered, breathless from her husband's affection. She lifted the package. "Your groom's gift."

"You are the only present I need." He squeezed her, his soft lips pressed against her forehead.

"I'll remember that come Christmastime." Jennifer laughed at Brett's quirked eyebrow.

He released her, taking the gift that she offered. "Will it break?" He put his ear close to the box, giving it a small shake.

Jennifer shrugged. "Open it and see."

"I like the paper."

Instead of wedding-themed paper, Jennifer had chosen a roll of wrapping paper meant for children. Various kinds of dinosaurs stood out on the bright yellow background. "I thought you might."

Popping the tape from one end, Brett ripped the rest of the paper off of the box in one fluid movement. Lifting the lid, he peeked inside. "This is the best gift ever." His laugh resounded around the quiet yard. He pulled out a black T-shirt with the image of Sue T-Rex across the front and *Chicago Field Museum* written under it. "I love it." He leaned toward Jennifer. She met his lips halfway.

"There's more."

Brett pulled a copy of *Transitions* from the bottom of the box. "You gave me a subscription to your magazine?" The puzzlement in his voice matched the expression on his face.

"Open it to page twenty." Jennifer laced her fingers together to keep from grabbing the magazine away and opening it herself.

Throwing the T-shirt over his shoulder, Brett leafed through the pages. His eyes roamed the page from bottom to top. A slow smile started gaining width. He looked over the magazine at Jennifer.

"The first official use of my new name." Jennifer bounced on her toes, and clapped her hands. The nonfiction article's byline belonged to Jennifer Lange.

"Look at that, I rescued you again." Brett winked. "I couldn't be prouder of you, and I know it will be the first of many."

Jennifer did, too. She had faith in her career decision.

"I'd rather stay here with you, but I think we'd better get down to the reception." Brett placed his hand on the small of her back, guiding her toward his pickup. He put his gift on the seat. In a quick, fluid movement, he lifted Jennifer into his arms, tucking her into the passenger seat.

The pickup bounced over the uneven ground past the pasture that now housed the buffalo herd. Their wooly winter coats loose and shaggy in the shedding stage for warmer weather. The white bison no longer visible in the crowd. Its coat turned brown during the winter months.

Brett eased around a jutted rock, and the dig site opened before them. The horizon, alight with crimson hues of the setting spring sun, brought out the rustic colors on the bluff from erosion's artistic brush.

Lighted camping lanterns lined the foundation that Brett's group had uncovered the previous summer. Inside the foundation's frame, a large white tent filled with friends and family welcomed them to their reception with a round of applause. Rounding the pickup to open Jennifer's door, Brett bowed to their audience. Jennifer slipped from the seat while Brett motioned to the guests for additional applause. Jennifer curtsied before everyone broke into laughter.

Guests approached them at the entry of the tent with congratulations. Jennifer saw her dad standing with Eldon and Cynthia in a back corner of the tent. With his hands in his tuxedo trousers pockets, no one would guess her dad only had about fifty percent of the use of his right hand.

"Excuse me." Jennifer left Brett with a group of his colleagues, making a beeline for her dad.

He held his arms open, the right slightly lower than the left. She embraced her father. "Thank you for all of this," she whispered.

"Anything for my little girl. You are as pretty as your mama was in that dress."

"Spitting image, except for those citified shoes."

Jennifer smiled. She turned to Eldon and Cynthia.

"Thank you, too. Everything out here is perfect." She looked around the tent. Lace tablecloths hung over the edges of round tables. Battery-operated candles that most people used to put in their windows at Christmastime sat in the center of each table surrounded by handpicked purple pasque flowers. A dream catcher, Cynthia's winter craft project, marked the place setting for each guest, their gift for helping Brett and Jennifer celebrate their love.

"It's what you do for your daughter." Cynthia patted Jennifer's shoulder. "And we're glad you'll be closer to home."

A warm thread of connection moved through Jennifer, letting her know she'd made the right choice.

"For a while." Brett wrapped his arm around her shoulders. "Come fall, we'll be taking our honeymoon."

"A *working* honeymoon in Belize." Jennifer patted Brett's chest before turning her attention to her family, hoping they caught her obvious show of pride for her husband's occupation.

Cynthia clapped her hands. "Your grant came through. How wonderful!"

"Congratulations on two counts." Matthew held his hand out to his new son-in-law.

"What are you going to do while Indy's out playing in the dirt?" Lance walked up beside them. He pecked a kiss on her cheek before holding his hand out to Brett.

Jennifer smiled at Lance's sibling teasing. Brett clasped his hand. Both of their knuckles grew white in a mock test of strength until their laughter erupted.

"I'm going to research landmarks, the culture, anything I think might be of interest to kids that would make a good nonfiction article that I can propose to magazines or book editors, similar to what I've been doing for the past year."

Jennifer had returned to Chicago before the July 1

deadline for the beauty editor position, to sublease her apartment. She'd called Jacque prior to leaving and pulled her name from consideration for the promotion. Working in a stuffy cubicle all day no longer held any appeal to her, not when she could accompany Brett to exotic locations.

"That's what Jennifer Lange will be doing. Jennifer Edwards will continue to give beauty advice through her monthly column at *Transitions*." The pride shining from Brett's eyes made her heart somersault, causing her happy smile to grow wider.

One short year ago, she'd asked for a sign from God that everything in her life would go back to normal. The sign that she received contained a different message. The white buffalo calf had caused her to reconsider her faith. Once she put her faith in God, everything in her life had fallen into place: her family, her career and love.

* * * * *

REQUEST YOUR FREE BOOKS!

2 FREE INSPIRATIONAL NOVELS
PLUS 2
FREE
MYSTERY GIFTS

Love Inspired

YES! Please send me 2 FREE Love Inspired® novels and my 2 FREE mystery gifts (gifts are worth about $10). After receiving them, if I don't wish to receive any more books, I can return the shipping statement marked "cancel." If I don't cancel, I will receive 6 brand-new novels every month and be billed just $4.74 per book in the U.S. or $5.24 per book in Canada. That's a savings of at least 21% off the cover price. It's quite a bargain! Shipping and handling is just 50¢ per book in the U.S. and 75¢ per book in Canada.* I understand that accepting the 2 free books and gifts places me under no obligation to buy anything. I can always return a shipment and cancel at any time. Even if I never buy another book, the two free books and gifts are mine to keep forever.

105/305 IDN F49N

Name _____ (PLEASE PRINT) _____

Address _____ Apt. # _____

City _____ State/Prov. _____ Zip/Postal Code _____

Signature (if under 18, a parent or guardian must sign)

Mail to the Harlequin® Reader Service:
IN U.S.A.: P.O. Box 1867, Buffalo, NY 14240-1867
IN CANADA: P.O. Box 609, Fort Erie, Ontario L2A 5X3

**Are you a subscriber to Love Inspired books
and want to receive the larger-print edition?
Call 1-800-873-8635 or visit www.ReaderService.com.**

* Terms and prices subject to change without notice. Prices do not include applicable taxes. Sales tax applicable in N.Y. Canadian residents will be charged applicable taxes. Offer not valid in Quebec. This offer is limited to one order per household. Not valid for current subscribers to Love Inspired books. All orders subject to credit approval. Credit or debit balances in a customer's account(s) may be offset by any other outstanding balance owed by or to the customer. Please allow 4 to 6 weeks for delivery. Offer available while quantities last.

Your Privacy—The Harlequin® Reader Service is committed to protecting your privacy. Our Privacy Policy is available online at www.ReaderService.com or upon request from the Harlequin Reader Service.
We make a portion of our mailing list available to reputable third parties that offer products we believe may interest you. If you prefer that we not exchange your name with third parties, or if you wish to clarify or modify your communication preferences, please visit us at www.ReaderService.com/consumerschoice or write to us at Harlequin Reader Service Preference Service, P.O. Box 9062, Buffalo, NY 14269. Include your complete name and address.

LIDIR13R

REQUEST YOUR FREE BOOKS!
2 FREE RIVETING INSPIRATIONAL NOVELS
PLUS 2 FREE MYSTERY GIFTS

Love Inspired.
SUSPENSE

YES! Please send me 2 FREE Love Inspired® Suspense novels and my 2 FREE mystery gifts (gifts are worth about $10). After receiving them, if I don't wish to receive any more books, I can return the shipping statement marked "cancel." If I don't cancel, I will receive 4 brand-new novels every month and be billed just $4.74 per book in the U.S. or $5.24 per book in Canada. That's a savings of at least 21% off the cover price. It's quite a bargain! Shipping and handling is just 50¢ per book in the U.S. and 75¢ per book in Canada.* I understand that accepting the 2 free books and gifts places me under no obligation to buy anything. I can always return a shipment and cancel at any time. Even if I never buy another book, the two free books and gifts are mine to keep forever.

123/323 IDN F5AN

Name	(PLEASE PRINT)
Address	Apt. #
City	State/Prov.	Zip/Postal Code

Signature (if under 18, a parent or guardian must sign)

Mail to the **Harlequin® Reader Service:**
IN U.S.A.: P.O. Box 1867, Buffalo, NY 14240-1867
IN CANADA: P.O. Box 609, Fort Erie, Ontario L2A 5X3

Are you a current subscriber to Love Inspired Suspense books and want to receive the larger-print edition?
Call 1-800-873-8635 or visit www.ReaderService.com.

* Terms and prices subject to change without notice. Prices do not include applicable taxes. Sales tax applicable in N.Y. Canadian residents will be charged applicable taxes. Offer not valid in Quebec. This offer is limited to one order per household. Not valid for current subscribers to Love Inspired Suspense books. All orders subject to credit approval. Credit or debit balances in a customer's account(s) may be offset by any other outstanding balance owed by or to the customer. Please allow 4 to 6 weeks for delivery. Offer available while quantities last.

Your Privacy—The Harlequin® Reader Service is committed to protecting your privacy. Our Privacy Policy is available online at www.ReaderService.com or upon request from the Harlequin Reader Service.
We make a portion of our mailing list available to reputable third parties that offer products we believe may interest you. If you prefer that we not exchange your name with third parties, or if you wish to clarify or modify your communication preferences, please visit us at www.ReaderService.com/consumerschoice or write to us at Harlequin Reader Service Preference Service, P.O. Box 9062, Buffalo, NY 14269. Include your complete name and address.

LISDIR13R

REQUEST YOUR FREE BOOKS!

2 FREE INSPIRATIONAL NOVELS PLUS 2 FREE MYSTERY GIFTS

Love Inspired

HISTORICAL
INSPIRATIONAL HISTORICAL ROMANCE

YES! Please send me 2 FREE Love Inspired® Historical novels and my 2 FREE mystery gifts (gifts are worth about $10). After receiving them, if I don't wish to receive any more books, I can return the shipping statement marked "cancel." If I don't cancel, I will receive 4 brand-new novels every month and be billed just $4.74 per book in the U.S. or $5.24 per book in Canada. That's a savings of at least 21% off the cover price. It's quite a bargain! Shipping and handling is just 50¢ per book in the U.S. and 75¢ per book in Canada.* I understand that accepting the 2 free books and gifts places me under no obligation to buy anything. I can always return a shipment and cancel at any time. Even if I never buy another book, the two free books and gifts are mine to keep forever.

102/302 IDN F5CY

Name	(PLEASE PRINT)

Address		Apt. #

City	State/Prov.	Zip/Postal Code

Signature (if under 18, a parent or guardian must sign)

Mail to the **Harlequin® Reader Service**:
IN U.S.A.: P.O. Box 1867, Buffalo, NY 14240-1867
IN CANADA: P.O. Box 609, Fort Erie, Ontario L2A 5X3

Want to try two free books from another series?
Call 1-800-873-8635 or visit www.ReaderService.com.

* Terms and prices subject to change without notice. Prices do not include applicable taxes. Sales tax applicable in N.Y. Canadian residents will be charged applicable taxes. Offer not valid in Quebec. This offer is limited to one order per household. Not valid for current subscribers to Love Inspired Historical books. All orders subject to credit approval. Credit or debit balances in a customer's account(s) may be offset by any other outstanding balance owed by or to the customer. Please allow 4 to 6 weeks for delivery. Offer available while quantities last.

Your Privacy—The Harlequin® Reader Service is committed to protecting your privacy. Our Privacy Policy is available online at www.ReaderService.com or upon request from the Harlequin Reader Service.

We make a portion of our mailing list available to reputable third parties that offer products we believe may interest you. If you prefer that we not exchange your name with third parties, or if you wish to clarify or modify your communication preferences, please visit us at www.ReaderService.com/consumerschoice or write to us at Harlequin Reader Service Preference Service, P.O. Box 9062, Buffalo, NY 14269. Include your complete name and address.

LIHDIR13R

ReaderService.com

Manage your account online!
- Review your order history
- Manage your payments
- Update your address

> ### We've designed
> ### the Harlequin® Reader Service
> ### website just for you.

Enjoy all the features!
- Reader excerpts from any series
- Respond to mailings and special monthly offers
- Discover new series available to you
- Browse the Bonus Bucks catalog
- Share your feedback

Visit us at:
ReaderService.com

Clint Nolan padded barefoot toward the front of the house as the doorbell gave an impatient peal. After spending the past hour fighting a stubborn tree root on the nature trail at The Point, he wanted food, not visitors.

Forcibly changing his scowl to the semblance of a smile, he unlocked the door, pulled it open—and froze.

It was her.

Miss Reckless-Driver. Kristen Andrews.

And she didn't look any too happy to see him.

His smile morphed back to a scowl.

Several seconds of silence ticked by.

Finally he spoke. "Can I help you?" The question came out cool and clipped.

She cleared her throat. "I, uh, got your address from the town's bulletin board. Genevieve at the Orchid recommended your place when I, uh, ate dinner there."

Since he'd arrived in town almost three years ago, the sisters at the Orchid had been lamenting his single state. Especially Genevieve.

But the Orchid Café matchmaker was wasting her time. The inn's concierge wasn't the woman for him. No way. Nohow.

And Kristen herself seemed to agree.

"I doubt you'd be interested. It's on the *rustic* side," he said.

A spark of indignation sprang to life in her eyes, and her chin rose in a defiant tilt.

Uh-oh. Wrong move.

"Depends on what you mean by rustic. Are you telling me it doesn't have indoor plumbing?"

He folded his arms across his chest. "It has a full bath and a compact kitchen. Very compact."

"How many bedrooms?"

"Two. Plus living room and breakfast nook."

"It's furnished, correct?"

"With the basics."

"I'd like to see it."

Okay. She was no airhead, even if she did spend her days arranging cushy excursions and making dinner reservations for rich hotel guests. But there was an undeniable spark of intelligence—and spunk—in her eyes. She might be uncomfortable around him, but she hadn't liked the implication of his rustic comment one little bit and she was going to make him pay for it. One way or another...

Will Clint and Kristen ever see eye to eye?

Don't miss SEASIDE BLESSINGS by Irene Hannon, on sale June 2013 wherever Love Inspired books are sold!

HEARTSONG

PRESENTS

Look out for 4 new
Heartsong Presents books next month!

**Every month 4 inspiring faith-filled
romances will be available in stores.**

These contemporary and historical Christian
romances emphasize God's role in every
relationship and reinforce the importance of
faith, hope and love.